Pamela Kavanagh was born in Chester, and later moved to the Wirral. On leaving school, she trained as a primary teacher. She took up writing seriously in 1990, and moved to Wales, where she took up spinning and walking. She now lives in South Cheshire.

THE PRIDE OF THE MORNING

1850s England: Emma Trigg has always accepted her grandfather's wish for a union between herself and her cousin Hamilton. Their marriage will ensure a continuation of the equestrian tack-making business on Saddler's Row, satisfy her aunt, and provide Emma with a secure future. But at Chester's Midsummer Fair, a chance encounter with personable horse dealer Josh Brookfield sparks a whole different chain of events. A friendship is severed, long-held secrets come to light, and Emma is drawn down an uncertain path. Can she ever forget the man with laughter in his eyes and the soul of a poet?

Books by Pamela Kavanagh
Published by Ulverscroft:

ACROSS THE SANDS OF TIME
THE LONELY FURROW

PAMELA KAVANAGH

THE PRIDE OF
THE MORNING

Complete and Unabridged

ULVERSCROFT
Leicester

First published in Great Britain in 2016 by
Robert Hale Limited
London

First Large Print Edition
published 2017
by arrangement with
Robert Hale
an imprint of The Crowood Press Ltd
Wiltshire

The moral right of the author has been asserted

*A catalogue record for this book is available
from the British Library.*

ISBN 978–1–4448–3192–4

For Hilary

1

A warning shout and the pattering rush of unshod hooves on the worn cobblestones of the street had Emma dodging aside to let a string of rough-coated ponies go by, the coper chirruping and cracking his whip energetically. Flattened against the crumbling cob-and-timber wall of a bakery shop, she waited until the road was clear and then continued on her way to the produce market, swinging her shopping basket as she went.

This was the Midsummer Fair and half the population of Chester seemed to be here. Merchants and traders jostled shoulders with fond mamas shepherding pretty daughters and gossiping clutches of housewives with small children in tow, all with an eye for a ready bargain. Under the towering sandstone walls of St Werburgh's, the usual stalls and booths had been set up and, early though it was, stallholders were doing a brisk trade.

Over the air, drifting from the Foregate where the beast market was held, issued the troubled whinnies and bellows of penned animals, the gabble of the auctioneer and the decisive thwack of the gavel. It had rained in the night and the reek of dung on sodden ground hung heavily in the atmosphere, laced with the sweetness of blooms from a flower-seller's speck at the entrance to the Abbey Square.

'Buy my fine lavender, missie?' the woman called out, her round, wind-buffed face crinkling up into a gappy smile. 'Marguerites, marigolds or pinks, as fancy takes you?'

Tempted, Emma selected a bunch of the lavender and inhaled its fresh scent, but shook her head and with a small sigh of regret returned the item to the wicker trug at the woman's feet. Her aunt did not hold with fripperies, and posies of flowers, according to the code of Maisie Catchpole, were just that.

As all this was taking place a tall figure in breeches and high boots, emerging from the Foregate with a coil of harness rope slung carelessly over his shoulder, caught sight of the pretty girl against the background of colourful cottage blooms and pulled to an admiring stop on the edge of the market place. For a long, still moment he stood there, looking at her, his eyes filling with a mild, uncomplicated interest.

Emma, totally oblivious to the attention she had created, tucked an errant strand of corn-gold hair into her bonnet and consulted her shopping list. Needles and thread. She would have to cross to the drapery stall for those. She hefted her shopping basket more securely onto her arm and set off through the milling throng.

She was almost there when a cloud sailed over the sun, plunging everywhere into shadow. Next moment, the rain began; a sharp shower that made Emma fear for her new bonnet, a fetching straw confection trimmed with ribbons of her favourite butter-yellow.

Around her, shoppers were scuttling for shelter. Emma was looking for a likely place when a voice said, 'Quick, this way!'

A sun-browned hand took her arm and she found herself being hustled through the deluge to a low stone archway that led into the abbey precincts.

'Bide here a moment. This rain won't be much — it's just the pride of the morning!'

The voice throbbed with good humour and Emma, anxiously testing her headgear for damage, glanced up into the deepest blue eyes she had ever seen. They twinkled teasingly in a lean, mobile face, and her heart gave a sudden bewildering lurch.

'I ... I don't mind the rain,' she stammered, finding herself at a loss and breathless. 'It's my bonnet that was the concern. It's new and I don't want it ruined.

My Aunt Maisie did warn me against wearing it today.'

'Is that so?' he said solemnly, though his eyes still danced.

As quickly as it had begun the shower stopped and the sun broke through again. Droplets of water sparkled in the speaker's mop of dark curls and the renewed warmth brought out a masculine reek that hung about his person; a not displeasing mix of horse, leather and green, open spaces. Something about him, the patched and work-stained fustian breeches and mucky boots, the flamboyant scarlet neckerchief at his throat and the coil of rope at his shoulder, suggested horse dealer and Emma, reminded of her Grandfather Trigg's words of caution on the subject, took a firm grip on herself.

'No doubt you'll be here for the stalls,' he went on sociably. 'It's business for me.'

'Horse business?' Emma prompted.

'That's right. I came with four and three have already gone, and the auction had barely begun. That's not bad at all. Means I shall be going home with a full purse.'

It sounded like bragging to Emma and her response was tart.

'Then I'd best not detain you, sir, or you may miss a sale on the fourth.'

He laughed.

4

'Oh, that would be of no consequence. There's always an outlet for a good riding horse. Besides which, it will give me something to get home on.'

'And if it does sell? What will you do then?' Emma asked him, curiosity getting the better of her. 'Walk home?'

'Nay, mistress, it's too tidy a step for that. 'Twill be more a matter of investing a portion of my earnings in another mount to sell on at the next fair. The name's Brookfield. Josh Brookfield.' She was sent a searching glance. 'And you are?'

'Emma Trigg,' she said, and then could have bitten her tongue. 'Is this what you do for a living, sir? It sounds a . . . a precarious life to me.'

'It's the best life ever. There's freedom in being one's own man. What's more, there are the horses. Do you like horses, Miss Emma?'

'Why, yes, I do.'

'There then.' Josh Brookfield clapped a work-callused hand in delighted satisfaction against his thigh. 'Didn't I know you were a girl after my own heart!'

He was too forward by far and Emma, blushing, looked for escape. Across at the drapery stall she could see a queue forming. She gave her companion a tight smile.

'Sir, I must take my leave. Thank you

kindly for your assistance.'

''Twas my pleasure, Miss Emma,' the horse dealer said.

She headed off to join the queue, conscious of that piercing blue gaze on her as she went. Her shopping list was substantial and by the time her basket was filled she had all but dismissed the incident. Lingering yet still, however, in a corner of her mind was a memory of intensely blue eyes laughing into hers, and a warm, engaging smile.

He had not seemed the rogue her grandfather professed his type to be. She wondered where he lived, if his yard was the usual hotchpotch of sheds and ramshackle barns attributed to dealers and the like, if he had a wife and babes to return home to . . .

At this point Emma collected herself and headed off along the Northgate and thence to Bridge Street for home. In her basket, as well as the household requirements, lay a twist of Granfer Trigg's best-liked tobacco, a pennyworth of the barley sugar her brother favoured, and peppermint rock for Hamilton, since he said it helped his indigestion. He had also confided a weakness for liquorice and she had added some as a treat. For Aunt Maisie there was a small bundle of lace.

It had cost Emma the last of her meagre

savings, and the gauzy length of sprigged muslin she had lingered longingly over had been discarded with a rueful shake of her head. It would have made a perfect gown for the summer, too.

She did not see the still, upright figure, observing her every move from the entrance to the Foregate.

*   *   *

Home was Saddler's Row, a series of slate-roofed, timber-framed buildings situated on an elevated and canopied structure of connecting walkways designed for the pedestrian in times gone by. The city Rows, as they were known, made progress less hazardous and a good deal more acceptable underfoot than venturing on to the bustling streets below, the churned and puddled surfaces made worse by the continued flow of horse traffic. The Rows also gave some degree of protection against the weather.

Trigg's Master Saddlers and Harness Makers was a dark little den displaying a wide selection of horse gear. Emma walked briskly past the brass-knockered front door of the house and gained access through the entrance to the shop, doorbell jangling rowdily.

Breathing in the familiar aroma of leather and cleaning oils, spiced with the tang of Granfer Trigg's pipe tobacco, Emma went through to the workshop where her grandfather was at his bench, alongside her brother, Alfie, and their cousin, Hamilton.

Gideon Trigg looked up from the set of driving reins to which he was attaching a gleaming brass buckle with practised stitches.

'Ah, there you are, lass. You've been gone a while. I were beginning to think you'd got lost.'

'Never.' Emma pecked a kiss on her grandfather's bewhiskered cheek. 'The queues today were endless. I vow they get worse every time. This is for you, Granfer.'

She dropped the twist of tobacco down amongst the scraps of leather and small tools on the bench. Then, since they were more or less promised, she went next to Hamilton and gave him the sweetmeats.

'And for you,' Emma said, turning to her brother.

'Barley sugar!' Alfie gave her a grin. 'Thanks, Em.'

For siblings there was only a passing resemblance between the two. Where Emma's eyes were a lively bright brown, an unusual combination with her fair complexion and blonde hair, his were hazel-green and dreaming and his hair was darker.

Emma adored her younger brother and thought him the best-looking man on Saddler's Row, though she was mindful not to let Aunt Maisie know that. For Maisie Catchpole, no one could ever compare with her Hamilton for looks, intellect or anything else she could call to mind.

Gideon Trigg cleared his throat noisily. His chest had troubled him again last winter and the wet spring and early summer had not helped any, either.

'Thank you for the baccy, Emma lass. Best you get through to the house. Your aunt were asking after you.'

'She'll be needing the fruit for the plum duff,' Emma said, and hurriedly divesting herself of cape and bonnet, she continued to the rear of the workshop, from which a narrow unlit passageway took her to the family's living quarters.

* * *

'Did you get everything?' Maisie Catchpole enquired from where she stood at the central kitchen table, up to her elbows in flour. She brushed the back of a hand across her over-warm forehead, leaving a smudge.

'Yes, Aunt.' Emma placed the shopping

basket down on the other end of the table. 'Will I put the things away for you?'

'If you please. You can leave the raisins and sultanas out. I shall need them shortly for the pudding. Was the fair busy?'

'Busier than ever. It rained too, just a little. It was lucky I found shelter.'

Maisie looked with suspicion at the heightened colour on her niece's cheeks.

'Your new summer bonnet. Is it spoiled?'

'No, not in the least.'

'I told you not to wear that bonnet,' Maisie went on aggrievedly. 'You know as well as I do how easily straw can turn to mush in the rain.'

She watched Emma bustle to and fro, putting this item in the larder off the kitchen, another in the dresser cupboard where the dry goods were kept; every move slightly impatient and somewhat chaotic, causing Maisie to wince when an item was carelessly dropped and had to be retrieved from the red and black quarry tiled floor — which had been scrubbed within an inch of its life that morning.

'Did you see anyone in particular, child?'

'No, Aunt.'

The response was swift and suspiciously breathless and Maisie's angular face sharpened. You never knew with these young misses, and with this one's background . . .

'Are you sure? You look a tad bothered to me.'

'I'm hot, that's all. What with the bread oven lit as well as the range it's like a furnace in here. Will I open the casement?'

'And let the flies in?' Maisie clucked her disapproval. ''Sakes, what are you thinking of, girl? When you've finished there you might stone the fruit for me. I'm all behind today. 'Twill be a miracle if I get the plum duff on the table by supper time.'

Shopping basket emptied, Emma came up and handed her a small package.

'This is from the fair for you, Aunt.'

First brushing the worst of the flour from her hands, Maisie removed the paper wrapping to reveal a length of buff-coloured cotton lace, ideal for re-trimming her best Sunday blouse. Her face softened.

'There, but you've a kind heart, Emma. Thank you, my dear. Really, you shouldn't go spending your money on me. 'Tis to be hoped you've got yourself something, too.'

'Oh, I've done well enough,' Emma said nonchalantly.

Stabbed by thoughts of prettily sprigged muslin and lost hopes, she tied on a voluminous white apron that swamped her slight figure, pulled a stool to the table and set about the irksome task of stoning and cleaning the dried fruit.

★ ★ ★

Later that day, the shop doorbell jangled. Gideon Trigg rose from his workbench and went through to the shop premises.

Standing by the solid oak counter that was pitted and scuffed from decades of use, was a tall young man with a shock of tumbling dark curls and a strong, outdoor face. Under his arm was a flattish parcel.

He gave the saddler a smile.

'Master Trigg? Good afternoon, sir. You won't know me, but I believe you've had dealings in the past with my father, Samuel Brookfield? I'm Josh. Father and I are in business together now.'

Gideon Trigg looked the caller over closely.

'You're Sam Brookfield's whelp? Aye, you do have a look of him. You've taken for your ma and all, about the hair and eyes, methinks. Irish lady, wasn't she? And a beauty to boot. Tragic that he lost her so young. Well, well, it's been a while since I set eyes on Sam.' He rubbed his bearded chin in thought. ''Twere before Victoria began her rule, if my memory serves me right — God save Her Majesty. How does Sam these days?'

Josh Brookfield's expression changed.

'I'm afraid Father's none too good, sir. He makes light of it, but he gets uncommonly short of breath and can't do what he used to.'

'Bless me, I'm sorry to hear that. Very sorry. Truth to tell I've never had much time for those of your persuasion, dealers and such, but Sam Brookfield's a man I'd trust with my last penny.' Gideon Trigg broke off. 'Now then, what can I do for you, young sir? Is it tack you're after? We've a goodly range on the shelf.'

'Fine quality, too, by the look of it. I shall certainly be paying the shop a visit in the future. In fact, I've come with this.' The parcel was dropped on to the counter top. 'I got talking over a jar at the alehouse with a fellow who has the drapery stall under the cathedral walls. Apparently a niece of a certain Mistress Catchpole of Saddler's Row had left this behind. Mistress Catchpole does reside here?'

'Aye. Her's my daughter.'

'And the young maid?'

'That'll be my granddaughter, Emma.'

'Perhaps you could see that she gets this parcel.'

'I will that. I'll not bother my daughter with it. Gets all of a heap over the slightest

13

thing, does Maisie. Well, her's not had it easy. Widowed young, and her not long wed. It were at the time my lad and his missus lost their lives of a sweating fever that were raging, leaving their two little'ns orphans.

'Maisie came here to housekeep and bring up the childer alongside her own lad, Mistress Trigg having long gone to her Maker and all.' Gideon Trigg paused, briefly reliving the sorrowful turn of events.

The caller looked on politely.

'But there, how I do go on.' The saddler made a gesture of apology with his hand. 'Happen you'll know some of this any road, from your sire.'

'Indeed, sir. Father speaks often of his long-term customers.' Josh Brookfield's face broke into a smile. 'Would it be yourself who drove a hard bargain over a ride-and-drive cob? Father laughs about it even now. Says he let it go for pittance in the end.'

'That would be Barney. The horse is getting a mite long in the tooth now. Mebbe the time's approaching to find something younger. Maisie's lad and Emma's brother need summat reliable to get about on and we use the trap for the deliveries, so a sound animal is a necessity.'

At this the caller's eyes narrowed in thought. Gideon hid a smile. They were all the same, these dealer fellows. Faintest sniff of a sale and they were on to you.

Sure enough . . .

'If it's a ride-and-drive animal you were wanting, Master Trigg, we may have the very thing. A handy grey. Five years old. Good to shoe, kind in the stall and sound as a bell. I've schooled him up myself. A more honest animal you couldn't wish for.'

Gideon considered. Old Barney truly wasn't up to the job anymore and the stable at the back of the house was big enough for two. Barney would do for light work, leaving a younger horse to undertake the heavier duties.

Happen too, that Hamilton might appreciate a visit to Sam Brookfield's yard in the Bickerton Hills. He could take Emma — it would be an ideal opportunity for the two young people to spend some time on their own together.

For sure as stirrups were stirrups, it was high time the pair were thinking of tying the knot. Gideon wanted to see the sign TRIGG AND CATCHPOLE go up over the shop entrance before he laid down his tools for good.

'Thinking on, lad,' he said to Josh Brookfield, 'I might well take you up on this. Only to look the animal over, mind,' he added. 'I'm not making any promises on a sale.'

'We are at your disposal, sir.'

The response came with such sincerity that Gideon warmed to the young fellow.

'Shall we say this coming Saturday, then? 'Twill not be myself calling, though I'm saddened to miss a chance of a jaw with an old friend. Another time, mebbe. It will be my grandson and granddaughter.'

'I shall have the horse ready,' Josh Brookfield said agreeably.

'Aye, do that. Saturday, then? Around mid-morning?'

'It will be my pleasure. Well, I'd best be off. You won't forget the parcel, sir?'

'No. Emma will be seeing to the horse about now. Spoils it, she does. I'll take this across to her right away. Farewell, lad. My regards to your sire.'

'Rest assured, sir, I shall pass them on,' Josh Brookfield said, and let himself out into the Row.

He was smiling as he walked away, his footsteps resounding on the wooden boards of the elevation.

* * *

Emma made for her room at the top of the house as quickly as she could, the parcel clutched to her. She had been startled by her

16

grandfather's description of the giver as he handed her the floppy package. Unaware of the turmoil within her, Granfer Trigg had ruffled her hair affectionately and proceeded to deliver a baffling and lengthy account of how the man had come by the item, but this Emma had scarcely heard.

Deep blue eyes and a merry smile? The young man in question could only be one!

In the privacy of her bedchamber, she ripped off the wrappings and let out a gasp of surprise. It was the sprigged muslin she had so admired on the drapery stall. Included for good measure were matching thread and a trim of narrow pale green ribbon that exactly matched the colour of the twining stems and leaves in the fabric. Tucked into the fold was a fragrant posy of lavender.

Emma's mind travelled back. She recalled standing, entranced, at the flower-seller's speck, admiring a trug of homely cottage blooms, picked with the dew still on them and sweetening the air with their perfume. Plainly, he had seen her.

She bit her lip. She could hardly accept so personal a gift from so casual an acquaintance. It was taking liberties indeed.

Then again . . .

Before she knew it she was loosening the folds of the material, draping it around herself, admiring the effect in the full-length looking glass of the tall polished mahogany wardrobe. What a lovely gown it would make, flounced and pin-tucked in the latest style, with the ribbon as a sash.

Downstairs in the hallway, the long-cased clock soberly chimed the hour. Aunt Maisie would be expecting her to help dish up the evening meal. She must leave this for now.

As she descended the stairs, an idea struck. Alice, her friend at the vintner's on Eastgate Row, would know what to do about the muslin.

Alice and Alfie had recently announced their betrothal. No date had been set for the wedding as yet, but Emma thought what a handsome couple they would be when the time came. She rather hoped that fun-loving Alice appreciated what an utter treasure she would have in Alfie.

★　★　★

It was later than usual when the family finally sat down to their meal, Maisie's face like a boiled beetroot from her labours in the broiling heat of the kitchen.

Everyone agreed on the excellence of the boiled fowl and duchess potatoes, and the plum duff and custard sauce that followed exceeded all expectations.

Supper over, Emma longed to get away but Granfer Trigg, it appeared from the huffing and clearing of the throat from the head of the table, had something to say.

'What I'm about to tell you has been in my thoughts for some while now. I've a mind to buy a new trap horse. We all know Barney isn't getting any younger and I've had a word with the co-owner of the place where Barney came from. He tells me they've got a ride-and-drive animal that might suit.' Gideon looked across the table at his grandson. 'Hamilton, you can take Emma there on Saturday and try the horse out for me.'

Hamilton frowned.

'This coming Saturday? What about that order we had for London Harness? I thought it was wanted in a hurry.'

'That's in hand. We can put in extra time of an evening. 'Twill help keep Alfie's mind off that pretty miss at the vintner's he's so taken with. Proper little flibbertigibbet she's turned out to be. Strikes me as Roland Courtney needs to keep an eye on that one.'

Maisie, with a glance at the two spots of affronted colour on Alfie's cheekbones, interrupted hastily.

'You were saying, Father?'

'Eh? Where was I? Ah, yes. What say you, Hamilton, to a jaunt up country?'

'I'm willing if Emma is. Where is this place, Granfer? It is a dealer's yard I presume.'

'Aye, a reliable one. This is Sam Brookfield's stable at Broxton in the Bickerton Hills. Traders, they are, more than dealers — 'tis a more respectable way of selling, to my mind. Seems as Sam Brookfield's lad, Joshua, is at the helm now. Josh, he calls himself.'

Emma swallowed hard. It looked as if fate were casting a hand here. No mention of the muslin, she was thankful to note.

As if in a dream she heard her grandfather concluding the arrangements for Saturday, heard her aunt's outpouring of distress at the prospect of sending her son and niece on what she considered a potentially dangerous mission, for wasn't it fact that the hills were rife with bands of ruffians lying in wait to relieve unsuspecting travellers of their gold?

'It were a couple of rounds of cheese off a farmer's cart, according to what I read in the newspaper,' Gideon dryly informed his daughter. 'Apparently a bunch of them make a point of rifling the farms for dairy stuff for a bit of lucrative trading. Didn't do them much good, bless me no! The ringleader's bound for the gibbet and the rest for deportation. I shouldn't worry your head, Maisie. Hamilton will take good care of Emma.'

Emma's mind went back to the muslin.

'Well,' she announced, 'if Alfie is going to be occupied in the workshop this evening I might give Alice some company myself. If I may, Aunt?'

'Of course, dear.'

'While you're there, Emma, you can ask Roland Courtney to send me another case of that Rhenish,' Gideon put in. 'Tell him to charge it to my account. I'll square up with him at the end of the month, as ever.'

'Very well, Granfer.'

Emma made her retreat before her grandfather could begin on another of the lengthy diatribes that all too often had the family sliding surreptitious glances at the clock.

★   ★   ★

'You met this young man at the Midsummer Fair?' Alice Courtney's slightly prominent light blue eyes widened. 'Oh, la! I was there with Mama and the only people we saw were ladies from Mama's afternoon-tea circle. So boring.'

She fluttered a small white hand to stifle a practised yawn, and went on to give her perfect coiffure a satisfied pat or two.

Much to Emma's despair, Alice was one of those fortunate souls whose red-gold ringlets never strayed out of place, whose gowns never betrayed a crease and who never left a stream of chaos in their wake. Unlike herself.

Take that morning, for example. Going out to collect the eggs from the small flock of hens they kept in the stable yard, she tripped on the trailing hem of her skirt that she had been meaning to mend but had not got round to seeing to. The egg basket had gone flying and so had the eggs. A similar encounter had taken place with the coal scuttle, spreading a gritty load all over Aunt Maisie's spotless quarry tiles. Aunt Maisie had not been best pleased.

'Emma, my pet, are you listening to me?'

Alice's voice cut into Emma's thoughts.

'What? Oh, sorry. Yes, of course.'

'You're like your brother, always daydreaming. Only it's verse with him.' Alice gave a throaty chuckle. 'He read me some the other night. Mr Blake, I think it was. Or was it Mr Browning?

'But there, I was saying, Emma,' Alice continued in more businesslike tones, 'you'd be foolish not to keep the muslin. It's what you wanted, is it not? Besides, how would you set about returning it? Go calmly up to this gem of a horse dealer and tell him you don't want his gift, right under Hamilton's nose? I vow he'd have an apoplexy, and his mama won't be there to kiss him better.'

'Oh, don't!' Emma said, giggling despite herself.

She was very fond of Hamilton, but whether her feelings extended to the marriage so desired by her grandfather she could not be sure.

It had been an assumption they had both grown up with, so familiar as to be almost dismissive. Now, she had pause for thought.

'You do like the stuff?' Alice said next.

'Well, yes. It's so pretty, tiny flowers and leaves on a white background. It would be perfect with my new bonnet, and I do so love this summer's shepherdess look.'

'Quite the little country girl at heart, aren't you?' Alice shrugged, and turned her attention to petting the soft-coated little Pomeranian dog on her lap, a birthday gift from her papa. 'Darling Suzette. You should have a dog, too, Emma. We could take them for walks together on the river meadows. It's a prime spot for riders. Two officers from the barracks went by yesterday.' She sighed dramatically. 'So dashing! My dear, you can't imagine how my blood raced!'

'Alice!' Emma was scandalized.

'Well, what of it? Just because I happen to be betrothed to Alfie doesn't mean I can't let my eye rove a little. Is your horse dealer handsome?'

'He's not my horse dealer. And Granfer says that the Brookfields are traders. Apparently there's a difference.'

'Trader, then. Dearest Emma, my sweet innocent, something has to have put those stars in your eyes and sure as nines it's not Hamilton . . . though I confess he does have a certain appeal. It's that boyish look of his — makes you want to mother him.' She paused. 'So what are you going to do?'

'Do?'

'My heart!' Alice rolled her eyes in despair. 'What are you going to do about the muslin?'

Emma shrugged.

'Make it up into a dress, I suppose.'

'I should think so too,' Alice said, smugly.

★   ★   ★

Towards the end of the week the weather improved. The sun was bright overhead when they set off on Saturday, the old horse heaving his weight into the shafts, his big hooves slowly negotiating the greasy cobblestones and mired mud of the town, the splodgy red-roan rump showing more grey

24

than Emma cared to see.

When she was a child she had prayed every night for God to keep Barney safe. Now in her twentieth summer she was more realistic, but made the request all the same.

She had taken pains with her appearance so as to compliment Hamilton's outfit of light grey broadcloth, immaculate linen and top hat, this being Aunt Maisie's instruction.

Or so Emma told herself. She had not missed the approving glance of the horse trader at her pretty high-crowned straw bonnet, and she made sure she was wearing it today. She had washed her hair in rosemary water and brushed it until it crackled and shone.

Her gown of sunny yellow exactly matched the colour of the wayside dandelions, some of which were turning to seed that drifted in gossamer fairy-clocks on the breeze.

They were out of the town now, heading along the Old Coach Road, a rutted highway that led eventually into the market town of Whitchurch.

'We turn left at the Feathers Inn,' Hamilton said, shaking the reins to wake the horse up. 'It will be several miles yet. Did you not bring a parasol?'

'No. I never thought to.'

'Alice would fear the sun playing havoc

with her complexion.'

Emma sniffed.

'Oh, phooey! Who cares about a few freckles? How come you know what Alice thinks, anyway?'

'I met her walking that little dog of hers and stopped to chat.' He darted Emma a smile. 'Why, I do believe you're jealous.'

'Of course I'm not.'

She squeezed his arm affectionately and sat back against the plush-covered cushions of the passenger seat, one gloved hand clutching the rail-guard against the bounce and sway of the four-wheeled gig, the other shielding her eyes against the sun's glare.

Leys of sprouting corn and lush red clover went rolling by, and grassy meadows in which sleek cattle browsed. The air was fresh and sweet, so different from the smoky fug of the city; Emma felt her spirits lift accordingly.

In due course they came to the turning and began the steady uphill haul along mazy lanes frothing with cow parsley and spikes of cuckoo pint. Sun-shadows chased across the rugged slopes of hills dotted with flares of golden gorse.

Hedgerows throbbed with birdsong and overhead a skylark trilled and trilled, as if it wanted the entire world to share its joy of living.

'Oh my!' Emma turned to Hamilton in open wonder. 'It's so lovely here.'

'Yes, it is,' he agreed affably. 'Though I dread to think what it's like in winter. We're better off in the town.'

'But I do so like the quiet. It's hard to believe there are bands of robbers here. I wonder where their hideout is. There must be caves somewhere.'

Hamilton shuddered.

'Don't even think about it.'

'You're right. It's far too pleasant a day for that.' All the same, Emma looked more searchingly around her. 'Have you the direction? We mustn't get lost.'

'Never fear, Emma. We'll be there shortly. Granfer said to watch out for the milestone to Larkton and turn onto a track. It's steep. It's to be hoped Barney copes with the pull.'

* * *

Soon afterwards the horse drew to a blowing stop in the stable yard. Emma looked about her with interest and a good deal of surprise.

Far from the ramshackle place of her expectations, this yard was neat and orderly. The roof of the stone-built stabling did not lack any slates and someone had recently been busy with the tar brush, for the woodwork gleamed blackly in the sunlight.

The heavy double doors were open to the air and in the stalls the rumps of the horses that could be seen, hind hooves resting contentedly, were glossy and muscled.

There was no lack of care here and Emma, whilst willing herself not to be cajoled by a pair of smiling dark-blue eyes, felt a rush of regard for the owner.

A welcoming hail made them glance round. From a low-roofed cottage the man himself emerged.

'Good day, ma'am, sir. You found us, then.'

'Indeed.' Hamilton jumped down from the high seat of the gig. 'Master Brookfield, I take it? Hamilton Catchpole at your service.'

The horse trader offered a strong brown hand and took the other man's in a grip that made him wince.

'Pleased to make your acquaintance, Master Catchpole. Shall I put your horse in the barn while you try out the youngster?'

'Pray do that,' Hamilton said curtly.

There was caution on both sides, Emma saw. Hamilton made no move to help her down so she opened the side door and was struggling with the portable step when Josh Brookfield took the initiative, and in a few deft movements had lowered it and handed her to the ground.

The physical contact, brief though it was, sent a jolt of emotion through her.

'My thanks, sir,' she managed to say.

'My pleasure, ma'am. Would you care to wait indoors? Father's there. He'd be pleased to furnish you with a cup of something refreshing to drink.'

Parched after the drive in the heat of the day, Emma was tempted. Granfer Trigg, however, would be sure to ask her opinion of the horse — besides which she was keen to look at the animal herself.

'Thank you,' she said, 'that would be welcome. But may I first see the horse?'

'Surely.'

Josh Brookfield gave her a nod and led Barney and gig away. Moments later he reappeared with saddle and bridle and took Emma and Hamilton into the stables.

In an end stall was a handsome steel-grey gelding.

'This is the horse I had in mind for Master Trigg,' the trader said as he tacked the animal up. 'He's a good-natured, tractable sort. I've not had a moment's bother with him. Of course, he's young yet and still has things to learn, but there's no vice in him, I can vouch for that.'

He led the animal out to a mounting block, tightened the girth and stood back to allow

Hamilton to mount, which he did, awkwardly. Emma patted the horse's arching neck, laughing as he lipped her palm in hope of titbits.

'He's lovely,' she said, standing back for Hamilton to enter a wide and grassy meadow to try out the animal's paces. 'Does he have a name?'

'He was already called Cygnus when he came so I've stuck with that.' She was given a shrugging smile. 'It's considered unlucky to change a horse's name.'

'Cygnus suits him. Is he good in the stable?'

'Aye, a perfect Christian.'

'That's a relief, since it's me who might have the care of him. Alfie helps when he can — Alfie's my brother. He says any horse in my hands has much to put up with. I'm not the most ladylike, I fear.'

'Depends what one considers a lady. From where I'm standing the prospect looks altogether acceptable.'

Emma felt her cheeks grow warm. They had moved to the rails to focus on the horse being cantered around the meadow with Hamilton a decidedly ungainly figure aboard its back.

'Did you get the package?' Josh Brookfield spoke without shifting his gaze from the rider.

'I . . . yes. Master Brookfield — '

'It's Josh.'

'I should not accept your gift.'

'Why not? Because it's not proper?'

'Now you're mocking me.'

His gaze slid to her.

'Nay, I'd not do that. Miss Emma, I acted with the best of intentions so where's the harm? You wanted the stuff, didn't you?'

'You were watching me!' Emma said accusingly. 'You sought me out at the shop.'

'Ah, but see what's come of it. A potential sale for the yard and a renewed contact between old acquaintances. Father was delighted to hear news of Gideon Trigg. You must let me introduce you to Father before you go — and partake of that refreshment if you so wish. Father would have come out to greet you himself, but his health is not good and this seems to be one of his less able days.'

'Oh dear.' Emma was grave. 'I'm sorry to hear that.'

'Aye, I believe you are, Miss Emma.'

He gave her a smile, which Emma found herself returning.

From the field came the uncontrolled scuffling of hooves and a shout as Hamilton urged the horse faster, and Josh looked up. This was obviously no horseman and the crude attempt to master the animal brought from the trader a quick intake of breath. He turned his attention back to Emma, his eyes very blue in his outdoor face.

'Do you like the fairs, mistress?' he asked softly.

'Yes, I do.'

'There's another at Frodsham come Saturday. They hold it every year and I vow it gets better each time. There'll be acrobats, troubadours, and horses aplenty to feast the eye upon. Aye, and tempt the pocket!'

He broke off, and then spoke impulsively.

'Come with me. Come and share the fun of the fair.'

'Me?' Emma caught her breath. 'Oh, but I couldn't.'

'Of course you could. You're free to come and go as you wish, aren't you? I'd meet you at a given place and have you back again afterwards, and no one any the wiser.'

'It . . . it wouldn't be seemly. My aunt would not approve.'

'You'll come to no harm. You have my word on that. Have you ever attended a fair for the sheer pleasure of it, Miss Emma? Have you never marvelled at the mysteries of the fortune teller? Laughed at the antics of the jesters? Tested your skills at roll-a-penny and toss-the-horseshoe?'

He broke off, and then said in a more beguiling tone, 'Have you ever danced to the fiddler as the sun goes down and evening sneaks across the fairground? They light the lamps then. It's a bonnie sight.'

Emma wavered, her mind reeling. Part of her, the demure, well-brought-up part, was berating the man for his nerve. Then again, some small ripple of adventurous spirit was surfacing with a sudden irresistible urge to fall in with his offer.

A day at the fair with an admiring young man at her side, away from the dull routines of the daily round, was oh, so very enticing.

Could she put her faith in him?

Yes, said a small inner voice decisively. Forward Josh Brookfield might be, but that steady gaze and honest expression inspired trust and liking. Would she be standing here had her grandfather not arrived at the same conclusion?

Emma was brought abruptly from her reverie by the sound of hoofbeats and Hamilton appeared at the field gate. He reined in, his face thunderous, light-grey eyes sparking in jealousy.

'Emma, what are you thinking of standing here in the glare of the sun? You know how easily you freckle. Do you want to return home looking like a gypsy?'

Emma was taken aback at his tone and indignation flared. She glowered at him, lips pressed tightly together. How dare he speak to her like that, and them not even betrothed yet! She was saved from giving vent to her feelings by an unexpected cry from the cottage. In the doorway a frail-looking old man was holding on to the door frame in obvious distress. He seemed to be gasping for breath.

Josh turned urgently to her.

'It's Father! Excuse me. I must go.'

He went sprinting off and Emma was about to follow when she felt a hand seize her arm, holding her fast. Hamilton had dismounted, thrown the reins over the gatepost and come to assert his authority.

'Emma, this is none of our concern. We've accomplished what we came for and now it's best that we go. Come along, let us fetch the horse and trap and be on our way.'

'But, Hamilton, that poor man. This could be serious.'

'Fie, Emma.' Hamilton was incensed, his cheekbones reddening, his brow furrowed. 'You would argue with me?'

Emma threw another troubled glance at the cottage. Josh was now at his father's side but the old man seemed on the verge of collapse. Help was required, and quickly.

Hamilton's grip tightened painfully, reminding her of her upbringing and the necessity of obedience. She looked in confusion from her cousin to the unfortunate tableau at the cottage door.

Dear God, what should she do?

2

'Sir, do let me help,' Emma said, breathless and flustered from the impulsive dash across the stable yard.

Leaving Hamilton glaring after her and probably in two minds whether to leave so young a horse inadequately tethered to the gate, she took Samuel Brookfield's arm and between them, she and Josh assisted him into the cottage and sat him down in a ladder-backed chair by a blazing fire — warm though the day was, Sam Brookfield evidently felt the cold.

To Emma's relief, the leathery old face which had been pinched and pale was starting to show a little colour. Even so, he was still fighting for breath and clutching his chest in discomfort, and she despaired to think that she had almost given in to Hamilton's request and left the scene.

'Have you a posset you can give him for these attacks?' she asked Josh.

'The doctor did prescribe something.' Josh was loosening his father's shirt collar, trying to support him in the chair, anything to give him ease. 'Father refuses to take it.'

'It might be worth trying. Will I stay with him while you get it? Oh, fie to this bonnet!'

Impatiently Emma yanked at her bonnet strings and flung the offending headgear aside. Designed more for fashion than comfort, her prized new bonnet was now restricting in the extreme.

Swathes of corn-gold hair tumbled about her shoulders, releasing a heady waft of rosemary, and Josh stared, momentarily taken aback.

Collecting himself, he went to rummage in a cupboard on the wall. Bringing out a slender purple glass phial, he sloshed some water from a pitcher on the dresser into a pewter cup and added a measure of the tincture.

With a little coaxing, they managed to get the remedy into the old man and gradually the wheezing abated. The pain seemed to subside; he sank back in the chair with a sigh.

'That's better,' Emma said gently. She reached for a bolster from a nearby settle and placed it behind his head. 'You lean back and rest. Don't try to talk just yet.'

She looked him over closely. The sinewy frame spoke of a once vigorous strength, and the weathered face under the thatch of white hair was kindly. It struck Emma how irked he must be by his condition and her heart went out to the man whom sickness had brought so low.

Josh came to stand beside her. In his hand was a brimming cup.

'The least I can do after your trouble is offer you some refreshment. It's Father's lemon cordial.'

'It was no trouble at all. I was pleased to help.' Now that the crisis was over Emma felt distinctly shaky. She accepted the cup gratefully. 'Thank you.'

'It should be me thanking you.' The smile was rueful. 'It devils me how you women cope in these situations. I must confess to panic.'

'Well, it's worse when it's your own kin.' Emma picked up the phial of tincture, inhaling. 'Foxglove. It has a bitter taste. Small wonder your father dislikes it.'

She was shot a look of quick interest.

'You are a herbalist?'

'No. I grow a few physic and household plants in the garden behind the house, but I'd need more ground to do it properly. I'd like a stillroom to work in, and little brown jars with cork stoppers. And a workbench and mixing bowls and a set of brass scales . . . '

Realizing her tongue was running away with her, she stopped, darting him a glance of apology under long lashes.

Josh's eyes warmed.

'You are ambitious, mistress. That is to be admired.'

'I don't think my Aunt Maisie would agree,' Emma said repressively.

A stirring from the invalid regained their attention. Shrewd, faded-blue eyes scrutinised Emma soundly.

'Lor' dumble us! I thowt I were seeing a ministerin' angel, what with that bonnie face and all that golden hair.'

'No angel, Master Brookfield. I'm Emma Trigg. Apparently you and my granfer are acquainted.'

'Aye, 'zactly so.' He frowned, brushing a fist across his eyes. 'Dang me if this room inna spinning like a top.'

'It's only the remedy doing its work. It will stop before long.'

'Dang stuff, making me twiddly in the head. And I've a thirst on me to parch the river dry!' Sam Brookfield paused to moisten his parched lips.

'Would you like a drink? A cup of this excellent lemon cordial?'

'I'd sooner a sup o' cider,' the old man growled.

'Don't listen to him, Emma,' Josh put in, laughing despite the situation. 'It's doctor's orders. No red meat, no strong liquor.'

'Him dunna know what's good, miserable old sawbones! I'd lay a pound to a penny as pretty Miss Emmie here wunna thwart a fella of his vituals.'

'No more would I,' Emma agreed stoutly. She gave him a beaming smile. She was liking Samuel Brookfield more by the minute.

'Emma, what's going on here? Are we to be all day?'

They turned to find Hamilton in the doorway. His face was grim.

'My apologies, sir,' Josh said. He retrieved Emma's bonnet from the floor where she had cast it, dusting it down before passing it to her. 'I'll fetch your horse and trap.'

Presently he was handing Emma up into the gig. Hamilton was making a great fuss of checking the harness straps and Josh, his expression safely guarded, took advantage of the moment to whisper, 'Saturday, then? Nine of the clock at the Dee Bridge.'

There was no time for response. Hamilton clambered up into the driving seat and with a sharp crack of the driving reins, sent Barney clattering away. Emma was conscious of Josh standing straddle-legged on the yard, watching her go, the sun glinting on his tousled mop of dark hair. Then they were through the gateway and trotting far too fast down the steep, rutted lane.

'Cousin, slow down,' she said in alarm. 'You'll have Barney slip and injure himself. Why the hurry? What's wrong?'

'We've dallied long enough,' Hamilton said coldly, though he had the grace to ease the reins. 'You'd no call to tender to that old man. It was not your place.'

'Oh, listen to you, Hamilton! You'd have me desert someone in need?'

'It made me look small, going against my wishes like that.'

'I don't think so. Poor Master Brookfield was hardly in a position to notice and neither was Josh.'

The name slipped out as a matter of course and Hamilton was quick.

'Josh? My God, Emma, you are too familiar by far! Whatever would Mama make of it?'

'My aunt would give me credit for dealing with the situation in the best possible way,' Emma replied in a tone that brooked no argument.

That said, she turned her attention to the scenery and Hamilton, visibly fuming, concentrated upon getting them home.

⋆ ⋆ ⋆

To Hamilton's chagrin, Emma had judged Maisie Catchpole's reaction correctly. As

41

soon as they arrived at Saddler's Row Emma went to change her clothes into something more suitable for seeing to the lathered horse, whilst Hamilton, abandoning the animal in his stall, sought out his mother to air his grievances.

The kitchen was full of the homely smell of newly washed laundry. Maisie looked up from wielding the smoothing iron over a cotton bed sheet, boiled to a startling whiteness and crackling with starch.

' 'Sakes, Hamilton! What a to-do. You have a fine summer's day at your disposal, a jaunt into the country with Emma — and all you do is grizzle because the girl out of the goodness of her heart goes to someone's assistance.'

'It wasn't that. It was the dealer fellow. He was flirting with Emma. She was smiling at him, encouraging him.'

'And you were struck by the green eye of jealousy. Well, that's no bad thing, to my mind. It shows you care about her.'

Hamilton's scowl deepened.

'Emma doesn't change. She's still the hoyden she was as a child. Her behaviour was deplorable. She'd cast off her bonnet and her hair had come loose. They didn't see me standing in the doorway. Brookfield was staring at her. You would not have been best pleased, Mama.'

42

Briefly Maisie's gaze flickered. Then she shrugged.

'The objective was to look at a horse for your grandfather. You had best go and tell him what you thought of it.'

'Emma will do that. Granfer's more likely to take notice of her than me.'

'It's true she has a good eye for an animal . . . Hamilton, where are you going?'

'Out. It seems nothing I say counts anymore.'

'But I've saved you some luncheon!'

His only response was the slam of the door.

Hamilton ran down the uneven stone steps of the Row and stood looking up and down the busy thoroughfare. It was early afternoon and everywhere heaved with horse traffic, townspeople going about their business and the usual assortment of pilferers, pickpockets and gangs of ragged street urchins. Which way to go? The quiet reaches of the river meadows beckoned.

Still piqued with Emma and upset that his mother had not taken his side, he set off, pushing his way irritably through the throng.

He was within sight of the Dee Bridge when, above the stink of city streets and the oily reek of the river, a pleasing drift of Attar of Roses assailed his nostrils.

Coming towards him, her pet dog under

one arm and parasol lightly held, was Alice Courtney. In her gown of speedwell blue with matching tussah silk pelisse and her high-crowned bonnet, she was the very breath of summer.

Hamilton raised his hat in greeting.

'Alice. Charmed to see you.'

'Good day, Hamilton.' She gave him a coy smile. 'What an unexpected pleasure. I thought you and Emma were out, some tale of going to see a horse for your grandfather.'

'That is so. We've been back this half hour.'

'Did all go well?'

'No, not exactly.'

'Oh dear!'

Her look was one of such utter concern that before Hamilton knew it he was unburdening himself into her sympathetic ear. The little dog closed its eyes and began to snore quietly.

Alice twirled her parasol, her light blue gaze intent upon Hamilton's face, her expression one of absolute absorption.

'Ah me,' she said, once the epistle had come to an end. 'In truth, dearest Emma can be somewhat headstrong. But there, we are not all made the same.'

'Indeed.' Hamilton was captivated.

Alice leaned closer; the scent of roses about her person was almost intoxicating.

'What a trying time you've had, Hamilton, dear. Would that I could help in some way.'

'Methinks you already have,' he said gallantly. 'I wonder, would you care to walk a little way with me? I was heading for the meadows.'

'Delighted, I'm sure.' She gave him a smile and it struck Hamilton what a fortunate fellow Alfie was to have won such a prize. 'If you would take darling Suzette for me?'

She deposited the furry bundle into his arms, which brought from the dog's throat a sleepy growl of disapproval. Warily tucking her into the crook of one arm, he offered the other to Alice and off they went, Alice chattering brightly, her heels tap-tapping along the road, the two of them heading towards the river together in the drowsy afternoon sunshine.

★   ★   ★

Sometime later, Alice welcomed Emma into the front parlour of her home on Eastgate Row. The room was stifling. Heavy plush drapes were half-drawn against the unlikely event of the evening sun glancing through the thick lace of the window-dressings and fading the soft furnishings.

A monster aspidistra plant wilted in an

ornate china bowl on the whatnot and fashionable porcelain figurines decked the marble mantelpiece and every other available surface, from the coy shepherdesses with smiling suitors beloved by Alice's mother, to Alice's favoured models of dogs.

Emma plumped down on the sofa, wriggling as the horsehair tickled the backs of her legs through the thin stuff of her clothes.

'Alice, such news,' she began, bending to pick up the Pomeranian who was investigating interesting smells on her boots.

'Give Suzette to me. Do continue, Emma. I'm all ears.'

'The outing ended in near disaster. Poor Master Brookfield, Josh's father, was taken badly just as we were about to leave. Hamilton wanted to go but I simply couldn't. So I went to help.'

'You entered the house? My oh my! What was it like?'

Emma frowned, thinking back.

'I really couldn't say to be truthful. I was too intent upon Master Brookfield. It's more a cottage, I think. Rather cluttered and dusty, but you'd expect that with two men. Anyway, I'm glad to say he recovered. But, Alice, before that, what do you think?'

'I cannot begin to guess.'

'Josh Brookfield asked me to go with him

to Frodsham Fair!'

'Oh, la!' Alice was agog. 'What did you say?'

'I turned him down, naturally,' Emma said in a voice as close to primness as she could muster.

Alice did not miss the note of regret in her friend's tone and was quick to pounce.

'My heart, Emma! Frodsham Fair is such enormous fun. Papa took me there last year, if you recall. It was where I bought that lovely gauzy shawl that goes with absolutely everything. You get the chance of going with a handsome young man and turn it down?'

'Well, what would you have done?'

'Why, accepted of course.' Alice's eyes narrowed cunningly. 'Did he say where to meet?'

'Yes, but — '

'Then you must go. Can you have the muslin made up in time?'

'I suppose so. Alice, I couldn't possibly. How would I get away for a whole day without them knowing at home?'

'Easy, you simpleton. I shall cover for you. You and I are spending the day together. The problem is solved.'

Emma bit her lip.

'I am tempted. I'd practically made up my mind on the way home. Hamilton was so disagreeable over my insistence on helping poor Master Brookfield it quite sickened me into a decision. But, well, I've had time to dwell on it since.'

'And your heart failed you. Fret not, Emma, my pet. After what happened today you deserve an outing. Take my advice and go with your horse trader.'

'I think I might,' Emma said daringly.

Alice hid a smile. With Emma removed from the scene she would be free to continue her delightful dalliance with Hamilton.

It was of no issue for her to deliver Papa's bill of sale for the Rhenish to Master Trigg. The gesture would provide the dual purpose of pleasing Papa and give her the opportunity to secrete a message to the right quarter.

After all, a girl needed a little excitement to look back on after she was wed.

⋆ ⋆ ⋆

'Hamilton, I've come to a decision over the horse,' Gideon said. 'I'm going ahead.'

Hamilton looked up from his workbench.

'An excellent choice, Granfer.'

'Aye. Thinking on, there's another excellent choice I want a word about. When are you and Emma announcing your betrothal? It ain't good enough to keep a maiden guessing.

With Alice Courtney and Alfie looking to beat her to the altar, she'll start to think she's left on the shelf.'

An unfathomable expression crossed Hamilton's face. He gave a small shrug.

'Emma is young in her ways. It may be wise to wait a while longer.'

'Poppycock! She'll grow up soon enough once you put a ring on her finger.' Gideon glanced round as the shop doorbell jangled. 'That will be the man about the London Harness.'

He made a mental note to have a word on the matter with Maisie when he could catch her alone, and went to attend to his client.

* * *

The opportunity to speak to his daughter arose that evening. Alfie had gone to see his intended. Hamilton was off on some mission of his own and Emma was upstairs stitching a new gown. For once they had the parlour to themselves.

'Maisie, I'll not beat about the bush. I want Hamilton and Emma betrothed before the summer's end. You can plan an Easter wedding for next year. How does that sound to you?'

Maisie speared her needle into the sock she

was darning and set her work aside.

'I'm not sure. Emma has many excellent qualities but she's still such a scatterbrain. I can't seem to drill it into her that she must take time to think before she acts.'

Gideon took a moment to draw deeply on his pipe.

'Oh, come now. Emma's impulsive I admit, but marriage and a full cradle will sort that out good and proper.' He paused, fixing his daughter with a serious look. 'That's not your only concern, is it?'

'No. Father, you know my thinking well enough.'

'Aye,' Gideon said heavily.

There was a long silence, into which intruded the sifting of coals in the grate and the slow tock of the clock in the hallway.

Gideon cleared his throat.

'Daughter, Emma's been with us since she were a nip of a child. You've brought her up to be God-fearing and mannerly, and that is what us must dwell on. You will speak with Hamilton? Tonight, when he comes in?'

'Very well, Father,' Maisie said with a sigh.

As soon as the clock struck nine, Gideon's habitual time to retire, he took himself off to bed. Some while afterwards, Hamilton appeared.

'Mama? You are late up. Is something amiss?'

'No, though there is a matter we need to discuss.' Maisie put away her mending and rubbed her eyes that were sore from straining in the light of the lamp. 'Your granfer has brought up the subject of you and Emma again.'

'Yes, he spoke to me earlier.'

'Best you do as he says, my love. You are fond of your cousin, aren't you?'

Hamilton fingered his top pocket in which rested an elegantly written missive secreted to him that afternoon.

'Of course I'm fond of Emma. She's my kin.'

'But not so close in blood ties to matter. Your granfer suggests a betrothal before the end of the summer and an Easter wedding. That is quite acceptable, surely?'

Hamilton was silent. He had liked being with Alice. Emma never looked at him the way she had, as if he was the only one in the world for her. It had made him feel strong and protective towards her.

He had enjoyed her bright talk that Granfer Trigg passed off as prattle. It had felt good, strolling along the river meadow with a fashionably dressed young woman on his arm.

Afterwards he had been swamped with regret that the interlude would not be repeated.

Then he had received the note from her . . .

He met his mother's gaze.

'Give me a few days' grace to consider the matter, Mama, if you will.'

'Very well, dear. Just bear in mind how pleased Emma will be to have everything sorted.'

★ ★ ★

The road into Frodsham rumbled and hammered with farm carts and gigs, fast-trotting riding horses and small, soft-pattering donkeys, as folk surged in for a day at the fair.

Josh, after attending to the horse and trap, took Emma's arm.

'This way,' he said cheerfully. 'Hah, see what's heading this way.'

Emma gazed in delight as a troop of jugglers in scarlet and saffron emerged from the throng and went capering past in a flurry of jingling bells and whirling hoops.

Ahead of them, a Punch and Judy show was drawing a lively crowd. The clamour of rhythmic footwork on wooden boards announced that somewhere, a clog dancing competition was in progress. There was the usual sale of farm stock and horses.

Aisles of gaily striped awnings adorned stalls offering a tempting array of wares; clothing, leather goods, silverware, brass and copperware and a bewildering selection of highly decorated bone china. Fairings abounded, some tawdry, others more select.

Sharp-eyed matrons shouldered their way to an area designated for foodstuffs and other household commodities, which Emma made a point of turning her back on. Home shopping was all she knew of these events. Maisie Catchpole had seen to that.

To judge by her escort's admiring glances, Emma knew she was looking her best. It had been worth sitting up at nights, transforming the length of muslin into the pintucked and befrilled gown that Alice decreed the very latest thing. Emma had even managed to fashion a reticule from a leftover scrap of material. Lined with silk from an old blouse, the prettily ruched creation made a handsome show on her wrist. And her straw bonnet, re-trimmed with the pale green ribbon to match her sash, finished off the outfit to perfection.

''Sakes, girl, you'll catch your death!' her aunt had said when Emma appeared at breakfast, ostensibly dressed up for a day out with her friend.

The pang of guilt the memory evoked was

soon forgotten, her attention caught by an organ-grinder with a small monkey wearing a tasselled cap and crimson jacket braided with gold. Whenever a medley of tunes came to an end the little creature removed his cap and held it out to collect the pennies that were tossed.

Emma clutched at Josh's sleeve.

'Oh, look. How clever! Do let's go and watch.'

Josh dipped generously into his pocket for Emma to make a reward. The gesture was acknowledged with a practised bow from the monkey, evoking murmurs of admiration from the onlookers and an avaricious glimmer on the part of the monkey's owner.

Next they attended the Punch and Judy, and then the clog dancing where rivalry was fierce. Noon was now approaching, food vendors shouting out their wares, and Josh bought them pies rich with meat and gravy, which they washed down with local cider from a man near the aisles.

The meal consumed, Josh turned to Emma.

'Where next? Shall we take a look at the stalls?'

'What about the horses?' Emma asked him, since she did not want to get in the way of business. 'I thought you were here to buy.'

He shrugged, dismissive.

'Too many gypsies here today. Gypsies bring good sound stock to trade amongst themselves, and stock that gives every appearance of being good and sound to sell to the public, if you see my meaning. Besides, I've a mind to make this a holiday, Miss Emma.'

'Then you'd best call me Emma, like everyone else.'

'Except Father. You're 'pretty Miss Emmie' to him. Seems you've made an impression there, Emma.'

On the journey here she had been pleased to learn that the old man had suffered no more attacks and was 'pottering about the place getting underfoot'. There had been no mistaking the relief behind Josh's words.

'See over there?' He pointed towards a small, brightly hued booth adorned with shooting stars, crescent moons and strange mystical symbols. 'A fortune teller. Why not go and cross her palm with silver? See what the future holds for you.'

Emma deliberated. At that moment a chill distinct wind blew, stirring the bunting that lined the street, setting the awning fluttering. It whispered coolly over Emma's warm skin and she shivered and shook her head.

'No, I think not. The future is best left to itself.'

'As you wish.' He looked at her closely. 'What a solemn moppet you are of a sudden. Happen a glance around the stalls will restore the smile. Shall we go?'

At the trade stalls he bargained soundly for a belt of tooled leather for his father, and deliberated over a set of harness on a stand piled high with horse gear, but to Emma's surprise turned it down in favour of visiting her granfer's shop.

'It's only right. After all, Gideon Trigg came to us for the horse,' Josh told her. 'Your turn next, Emma. What is it to be? A pretty shawl? A fairing to take home with you?'

'Oh but I couldn't.'

'Of course you could. 'Twill be a memento of the day — and I vow I know the very thing.'

He took her by the hand and guided her, laughing in protest, through the press of fairgoers to a small stand dealing exclusively in jewellery. There was nothing tawdry about anything here, no beads of coloured glass or worthless tin brooches or other bits of trumpery that generally passed for a fairing. From the glittering wares on display, Josh selected a delicate silver-link bracelet bearing five tiny charms: a church, wedding slipper, cottage, spinning wheel and a cradle.

'Tes known in the trade as a maiden's wish

56

trinket,' the stallholder informed them with a knowing smile.

Warm colour flooded Emma's cheeks, but Josh was intent upon investigating a dish of loose charms and did not notice.

'Ah, this is the one,' he said at last, and having found what he sought he asked the stallholder to add it to the chain.

It was a figure of a little cantering horse.

Once the charm was attached, Josh fastened the bracelet on Emma's wrist.

'Wear it always,' he said. ''Twill bring you luck.'

Apart from a much treasured cameo brooch in an ornate gold setting that had been her mother's, Emma possessed no other jewellery and the gesture took her breath away.

'Oh, but it's beautiful!' she whispered. She looked up at him with such rapture that on impulse Josh bent and pressed a kiss on her lips. The flame that roared through them both was unexpected. Josh drew back in surprise and the blush that had stained Emma's face drained away, leaving her pale and inwardly shaken.

Josh was the first to recover.

'Is that the players I hear tuning up? Do you like to dance, Emma? Of course you do.'

The bracelet came with a slender draw-string pouch of tussah silk which Emma conveyed to her reticule, after which she was whirled away to where a jaunty band of country musicians were already pulling the dancers onto the floor.

Time sped by and it was later than intended when Josh finally dropped her off at the Dee Bridge at Chester. Aware of a confusion of emotions, Emma watched him drive away before transferring the bracelet from her wrist to the protective pouch, which she then concealed under her bodice.

No one must know. No one.

She headed off for home. As she was passing the entrance to the river meadows she glimpsed a pair of lovers kissing in the moving shadows of the chestnut trees, clad now in the heavy leaf of full summer.

One of them was Alice and Emma naturally deduced that her companion was Alfie. It was not until he raised his head that she saw it was not her brother at all.

It was Hamilton!

★ ★ ★

'I saw you!' Emma said accusingly.

She stood her ground on the highly coloured carpet of the vintner's parlour, a fiercely indignant figure, her chest heaving and brown eyes filled with hurt. 'You were kissing. Alice, how could you? What about Alfie?'

Alice, relaxing on the cushioned sofa, lifted a taffeta-clad shoulder in a shrug.

'Alfie is not going to find out. You're saying nothing and Hamilton certainly won't.'

'You don't care, do you?' Disbelief rang in Emma's voice. 'You planned this — to get me out of the way and make a play for Hamilton.'

'It was a dalliance. A spot of fun. Like you and your horse trader.'

'It is not the same. You are promised to my brother.'

'So I am.' Alice left off stroking the dog on her lap. Her eyes narrowed warningly. 'And so I shall remain, because if some little bird goes telling tales then I shall have a bigger tale to tell. Do I make myself clear?'

Emma's hand flew to her throat in alarm.

'Alice, you wouldn't! You're my friend. Leastways, so I thought.'

'You're having doubts?'

'Indeed I am.' Emma's voice shook. 'How can we ever be friends again?'

'Dear me.' Alice affected a yawn behind the back of her hand. 'You must learn to be more worldly, Emma.'

Emma looked at Alice with something close to revulsion.

'Alice. I trusted you. I can never trust you

again. I . . . oh, enough of this.'

She turned on her heel and left, giving the front door of the house such a slam that the dog sprang to the floor and barked for all she was worth.

★ ★ ★

Emma was in turmoil. Her friendship with Alice was in ruins, her brother's pending marriage was a cause for concern, and now Aunt Maisie was pressing for a betrothal date with Hamilton, when Emma could scarcely bring herself to speak to him, let alone agree to be his for life.

Her mind swung to Josh. His kiss, brief as it was, had awoken unimaginable emotions in her. Had he felt the same? Or was he what Aunt Maisie would have called a philanderer, one who played on others' feelings and then abandoned them?

Perhaps, she thought, it was best to remain living quietly here under Granfer Trigg's roof, helping with the daily round and trying to school her clumsy efforts into the polished ways her aunt insisted befitted a young miss.

In the privacy of her bedchamber Emma would take out the bracelet and look at the charms, each a novelty in itself. The church opened up to reveal a bride and groom at the altar and the cottage roof also lifted to show a cosy scene within. The cradle contained a baby; the wheel turned on the spinning wheel. Each one was a joy, but in her heart she treasured the little cantering horse the most.

'Wear it always,' Josh had said. No further word had come from him and as the days went by Emma deduced that she would be naïve to expect it.

All the same, she wore his gift in its silken pouch on a narrow ribbon around her neck, concealed under her clothes.

★　★　★

Emma was out shopping with her aunt when Josh Brookfield delivered the new horse.

'Decent young fellow,' Gideon announced at supper that night. 'He invested some of my payment in a set of harness. That's what I call good trading.'

Memories surfaced in Emma's mind: the glint of sunlight on burnished dark hair, the brush of warm lips on hers. Jangly music, dancing feet, the feel of strong arms about her. She bent her head demurely over her plate, trusting that no one noticed the heightened colour in her cheeks.

Business at the saddler's shop was thriving and as a rule it was Alfie or Hamilton who dealt with the deliveries. Several days later, however, all three men were engaged upon a rush order and it was left to Emma to deliver a side-saddle to a house a few miles away at Waverton.

Cygnus had not yet been out of his stall and was fresh, fidgeting as she fastened the traces on the harness, tossing his head impatiently when she climbed into the gig. She took up the reins and drove him out of the yard, holding him back with difficulty until a suitable gap appeared in the clot of slow-moving traffic on the main street. Jinking nervously, Cygnus took her along the unaccustomed city thoroughfare, his eyes showing the whites behind his blinkers, neck arched like a coiled spring.

Once out of the town, she was able to give him his head. The young horse went eagerly, trotting out with more confidence along the quieter and less bewildering country lanes, the gig bowling along in the sunshine. Emma started to relax.

All went well until they came to a pair of cottages. They were passing the gates when a dog bounded across one of the gardens, ducked through a gap in the hedge and ran snapping at the horse's hooves. Cygnus let out a snort of fright, baulked violently and took off!

'Whoa! Cygnus, stop!'

Emma shouted, fielded the reins as best she could, all to no avail. She braced herself against the back of the seat and tried to pull him up, but Cygnus's jaw was set. He went thundering on, oblivious to hands and voice, the gig bouncing perilously over the rutted surface of the road.

Emma's bonnet fell back. Her arms ached with effort. The reins were useless in her hands, her throat dry from shouting. The wayside hedges rushed past in a haze of dusty green and brown. They seemed to be hurtling towards destruction and in the end Emma closed her eyes and prayed.

★　★　★

Josh was returning from a sale, the moneybag at his belt satisfactorily full. His father had not looked so good that morning and Josh urged his mount on, anxious to see that all was well and to share the glad news of the day's trading with him. A boost in business usually restored the sparkle to the old trader's eye.

He had reached the crossroads when his gelding's ears pricked alertly, and then Josh heard it too; the unmistakable rattle and clamour of a bolting horse and carriage. Next moment the culprit came into view. There was no doubting the pounding dark-grey shape between the shafts and the cloud of loosened golden hair of the driver.

'Come on, boy!'

Josh clapped his legs against the gelding's sides and sent it galloping in pursuit. By now Cygnus was tiring and they quickly caught up with him. Galloping alongside, Josh reached for the reins and was able to bring the wild flight to a halt.

Runaway horses were nothing new to Josh. He gave Emma a wide grin and said with due lack of concern, 'Ho there, Emma. We meet again!'

Then, taking in her dishevelled appearance and white face, the frightened trembling she was doing her best to control, his heart softened.

'Are you all right?' he enquired in gentler tones.

'Thank you, yes. A dog spooked him. My hands went numb, or I would have pulled him up myself.'

'Of course you would,' Josh agreed soberly. Both knew it was bravado speaking. 'Emma. This is a young animal, reliable under saddle but not long broken to harness. He needs time and a firm hand. I did point that out when you came to see him. What was your grandfather thinking of, letting you drive him on your own?'

'Granfer expects me to manage. It wasn't the horse's fault. He'd been shut inside when he obviously needed exercise. I thought it best to let him get used to his new surroundings before taking him out. It seems I was wrong.' She paused, and then finished falteringly, 'It looks as if I shall have to ride him out every day.'

Josh had no idea what made him make his next move, especially since he had vowed to concentrate his energies into furthering the business and never to come under the spell of a pretty face. Yet make it he did.

'Emma, I ride my horses out first thing. What if we arrange a place to meet? I could help you with Cygnus, just until you get the measure of him.'

She made no answer. He saw the agony of indecision in her bright brown eyes.

'Dawn tomorrow? Here, at the crossroads?' he pressed.

From the mere across the way a pair of swans rose in graceful flight.

Two for joy, Josh thought, and was unprepared for the bolt of emotion that shot through him when Emma gave a small nod.

'I'll be here,' she said breathlessly.

3

Emma leaned forward in the side-saddle and gave Cygnus his head, laughing as he broke into a gleeful gallop, hooves thudding on the stony uphill track, steel-grey mane flying back into her face. Over the summer her confidence had grown and she sat the horse fearlessly, glancing ahead to see if Josh was there.

Not for the first time she wished she had a more becoming riding habit to wear, her old emerald plush being past its best. Once, she could have approached Alice for a dip into her plentiful wardrobe, but the unfortunate rift had not been breached and she felt again the aching sorrow of friendship lost.

Josh was there as always, waiting in the shadow of a stand of tall pines, a motionless figure on a big black horse — a recent acquisition and one he had claimed for his own.

'Emma,' he greeted as she reined in, smiling and rosy-faced, beside him.

Black Diamond sidled spiritedly, eyes showing the whites, and Josh took a moment to give the stallion's arching neck a calming stroke before continuing.

'I watched you coming up the track. You manage Cygnus well now.'

Emma's heart lurched. She lived for the dawn gallops when she could be with Josh. She wanted the summer to go on for ever and went in dread of their meetings drawing to an end. Carefully, she phrased her response.

'Not always. Cygnus still tries to make off with me when he has a mind to.'

'The deuce he does!' Josh's eyes twinkled. 'Mayhap he needs the tickle taking out of his feet. Have you to be back promptly today?'

'No, not especially. My aunt is out visiting friends and the men are at work. I'm to get the luncheon, so providing I'm home by then the morning is mine.'

'Well then, how about a ride to the yard? Father's been asking after you, and the bay mare has foaled. It's a filly. You might care to see her.'

The foal was much awaited. Josh had confided his plans to broaden the business and breed a few handy animals himself. He had gone seriously into the bloodlines of his choice and was banking on a filly for affinities, always supposing the result came up to expectations. The need for being selective was paramount.

'A filly?' Delight blazed on Emma's face.

'Oh, I'd love to see her.'

'Then let's go.'

The horses fell into dancing step, with Josh ever mindful to keep to the hidden raikes and lanes, away from the main highway where they might be spotted together.

'How does your father?' Emma enquired as they jogged along.

'Could be better. I grow more concerned for him. I don't like leaving him on his own for any length of time, though I fear I shall have to before long. There's an auction I must attend on the coast. It's at Parkgate.'

'Why, that's where Alfie and I come from. I was eight when Mama and Papa passed on and remember it well. Alfie's younger. He doesn't recall much at all.'

'What a sad affair to lose both parents. What happened to them?'

'They took a fever that was raging. 'Twas rumoured it came off the ships.'

Memories surfaced as they always did, thrusting her back into a time of terrible loss and anguish. Conscious of Josh reaching out a hand in silent commiseration, Emma snatched her arm away, jerking the rein in the process so that Cygnus threw up his head with a noisy rattle of bit and curb chain.

'What is it?' Josh said.

'I . . . nothing.'

She met his puzzled stare and looked quickly away. How could she explain that his very touch was both sweet and bitter to her? That what she felt for him was more than mere companionship. There were times, daring, rose-tinted times, when she allowed herself to dream that Josh, not Hamilton, was the focus of the forthcoming marriage plans at Saddler's Row. Her initial attraction for him had deepened slowly, irrevocably. Hamilton she loved and respected as her cousin, but what she felt for Josh was different in every respect. He had claimed her heart in a way that Hamilton never would.

She had said nothing to Josh about her betrothal. All that was another world, far removed from this joyful escapade with the man with the blue Irish eyes and the soul of a poet, who looked upon a simple rain shower as the pride of the morning.

'Shall we gallop?' Josh shortened his reins. 'Let's see if Cygnus can keep up with Black Diamond.'

Emma took up the challenge and the horses sprang forwards. The pace was good and very soon they were entering the trader's yard, the horses snorting and tossing their heads, sweat glistening on their necks and flanks.

'I'd best walk them round to cool them

off,' Josh said, dismounting.

He went to help Emma down. She kicked her left foot from the stirrup and brought her right leg over the high pommel of the side-saddle, enduring the sweet torment of strong hands about her waist as she was lifted to the ground.

First and foremost was a call at the cottage to see Sam Brookfield. To her concern Emma found him in his chair by the fire, wheezing badly, his pallor more pronounced than ever.

'Sir, how are you?'

'All the better for seeing you, Emmie.'

'Flatterer! You seem a mite out of sorts to me.'

'Aye, well, I just gets all over twiddly at times.'

'Dear me. That won't do at all.' Emma knew how he disliked fuss and kept her tone light. 'Are you taking the tincture I made up for you?'

'Oh, aye, Josh sees to that.'

'You must take it regularly, three times a day. And don't forget the poppy juice at night. 'Twill help you sleep.' She gave him a smile. 'Well then, let's get this room sorted. I vow there's more straw in here than in the stable!'

Many visits had been made here since that day in June and the cottage felt almost like a second home. But where housework at Chester was a chore, tidying up after Josh and his father brought a curious sense of satisfaction. Keeping up a bright chatter, Emma removed her tricorne hat that had long since lost its swathe of emerald chiffon, and went through to the scullery to fetch a broom.

★ ★ ★

By the time Josh arrived from attending to the horses the floor was swept, the pots washed and the fire refreshed. Emma and his father sat drinking tea.

'You shouldn't trouble yourself with all this clearing up,' Josh said to Emma. 'We're used to a speck or two of dust here.'

'Dunna you heed him, lass,' his father put in, 'it does me good to see the place being titivated a bit. Takes me back to when the missus were here. Tes years since my Kathleen passed on, and Josh nobbut knee high to a grasshopper, but not a day passes that I dunna think of her. Lovely, she were. Dark hair and eyes so blue you felt you were drowning in their depths. Josh has a look of her. Pity him dunna shape up and take a wife like her to see after him. I could die easy then.'

The implication was clear and Emma blushed hotly.

'Let's hear no more talk of dying,' she chided him, before turning to Josh. 'Tea?'

'Aye, thanks. Then you must come and meet the new arrival.'

* * *

Mare and foal stood on a deep bed of straw in a corner of the foaling box. Leggy, with delicately curved ears and a little tuft of a tail, the foal gazed innocently back at Emma.

'Oh, but she's lovely! You are keeping her?'

Emma turned a rapturous face to Josh and something caught at him, poignant and unexpected. He had thought he had his emotions safely under control, but plainly this was not so and finding himself at a loss, his answer was bluffer than he intended.

'For now, certainly. Depends how she shapes up. I never was one anyway for sending mares and newborns to the auction. It seems cruel practice, to me. A foal needs to feel the fresh grass under its hooves and the sun on its back. I shall be turning these two out in the meadow for what's left of the summer. Then, we shall see.'

He paused.

'How did you find Father?'

'Not good, I fear,' Emma said gently. 'Is the motherwort potion not helping any?'

Josh shrugged. Excellent though the healing properties of herbs were — and Emma had proved herself skilled in their usage, providing a cure for an ailing horse and a salve for himself, when a cut on his hand had festered — they both knew in their hearts that in this case it was a losing battle. Sam Brookfield's days were numbered.

'I could try hawthorn,' Emma continued, lost in thought and frowning. 'I have a free hand nowadays in the still-room, what with my aunt being occupied with the nuptial plans.'

She broke off, a guilty flush touching her cheekbones.

'Nuptial plans?' The jolt that went through Josh shook him.

He listened, grim-faced, to her stumbling explanation. She was to be betrothed at the end of October and wed on Easter next.

'You are to be married?' he said, hearing the disbelief in his own voice and powerless to do anything about it. 'Emma, you've never said.'

'No,' she agreed woodenly.

Josh stared at her, his mind racing. Part of him, a small unworthy part, registered the fact that the revelation had its merits. He and

73

Emma had grown perilously closer over the summer. It had developed subtly, creeping up on him. This new turn of events should have given him grace and he waited for the rush of gratified acceptance that did not come. All he felt was an aching sense of loss, pierced by a stab of envy for the man who had won her hand.

'Who is it?' he asked savagely.

'My cousin Hamilton.'

'Hamilton Catchpole? They're tying you to that milksop? Deuce!'

Josh thought back, his conscience panging. He had flirted with her, dammit. Kissed her even, that day at Frodsham Fair. What man wouldn't have? And all the while she had been part-promised to another. Had he known, he would never have taken advantage.

One thing was certain. The dawn meetings must cease, for Emma's sake. As the betrothed of another man, her reputation had to be above reproof. He must make that clear and in doing so make the transition of getting his own life back on an even keel. He had managed without her before, hadn't he?

She was looking at him with fear and uncertainty in her brown eyes. On her wrist she wore the trinket he had given her and she twisted it round and round in agitation.

'Catchpole!' he repeated in disgust.

Disquiet throbbed on the air and the mare threw up her head in alarm and nudged her foal warningly. Brought at once to his senses, Josh caught Emma's arm.

'Come, we're upsetting them. I'll see you home.'

'You don't have to accompany me,' she told him sadly.

He snorted.

'Poppycock! These parts are not safe for a female travelling alone. Of course I shall see you back safely. And Emma, in the light of what you have just revealed, it is obvious that this must be your last visit here. You and I shall not continue with these early morning trysts. You are competent anyway with the horse, so let this be an end to it.'

He hustled her out into the sunlit stable yard and left her there, silent, while he fetched the horses.

Josh felt bereft, as if the sun had gone and storm-clouds were gathering. He told himself it was for the best, but a small inner voice begged to differ. What a fool he had been not to have guessed there was an understanding between Emma and the cousin when they had come here together that day in June. What a blinkered, self-centred fool.

★ ★ ★

Emma was surprised and a little disconcerted to find Alfie waiting for her in the Saddler's Row yard.

'You've been gone a long while,' he said as he helped her down from the saddle. 'I heard you leave at dawn.' He looked at her searchingly. 'What's happened, Em? You're different lately. Dreamy, abstracted.'

Emma opened her mouth to speak but tears choked her throat, and next moment she was weeping bitterly into the rough fabric of her brother's brown fustian jacket that smelled familiarly of leather and saddle oil and Granfer Trigg's pipe tobacco.

'It's Josh Brookfield!' She gave a gulping sob. 'He came to my rescue when Cygnus bolted with me. He offered to help me with him.'

Gradually, the story unfolded.

'Alfie, I love him so much and now I'll never see him again,' she finished on a wail of despair.

Alfie gave her shoulder a comforting pat or two.

'Perhaps it's better so. You were taking a risk. If anyone were to find out — '

'Nobody would have. Josh made sure we weren't seen together.'

'I don't doubt it,' Alfie said wryly. He handed her a kerchief from his pocket. 'It's all to the good that Brookfield has made a stand. You'll see that once you've got over your disappointment. Think of Hamilton. I daresay he has his faults but he's not a bad fellow at heart.'

Emma scarcely heard what was being said. All she could think of was the cold fury in Josh's eyes that had made the blue deepen almost to black when her secret was revealed. Fury, and some other emotion she could not identify.

'Emma,' Alfie then said, his voice deadly serious. 'I need your advice.'

'Oh?'

'It's Alice. She's become indifferent towards me and I can't think why. Has she said anything to you?'

Emma bit her lip. She badly wanted to tell her brother about Alice's penchant for minor flirtations, but she could not bear to see him hurt. She recalled having spotted Alice and Hamilton together. At the time she had made allowances. Once their betrothal was forma-lised Hamilton would be true to her, she had told herself. Besides, had she not indulged a hopeless fantasy herself?

'I haven't spoken to Alice in weeks,' she told Alfie. 'We had words, I fear.'

At that moment the town clocks began to chime the noontide hour and effectively released Emma from further explanations.

'I must stir myself and prepare the luncheon. Try not to worry, Alfie. Alice loves you really. How could she not?'

She led the horse into his stall, hoping heartily that her words would bear fruit.

* * *

Hamilton sighed. What to do about Alice? There had developed a more serious edge to their liaison and he had no idea how best to deal with it. He liked Alice tremendously, perhaps loved her.

Romantic love, in his view, was all tied up with wedding bells and orange blossom which soon became reality once the babies started coming along.

Could he visualize Alice as a mother?

Possibly, considering the billing and cooing that went on over the pet dog.

On the other hand, plans were being made to bind him to Emma. What a pickle it all was. What a blessing his mother had not caught on . . .

Hamilton, unfortunately, had underestimated Maisie Catchpole's powers of observation.

During the afternoon he escaped to the kitchen for something to satisfy his sweet tooth and help take his mind off his worries, and found his mother putting the finishing touches to an eel pie — a favourite of his grandfather's.

'There's a raspberry sponge in the larder,' she said to his request. 'It's for tea, so mind you leave enough.'

Maisie watched as he helped himself to an over-generous slice of the cake, her eyes narrowing shrewdly.

'Hamilton, I wasn't born yesterday. What's amiss?'

'Not a thing, Mama. Why should there be?'

'Oh, don't play the innocent with me. 'Sakes, I have to wonder what's happening here. There's Alfie preoccupied and Emma downright morose. As for you, well, if there is anything wrong, then you'd best say.'

Hamilton hesitated, and then spoke in a rush.

'In fact, Mama, it's Alice. Alice Courtney.'

Maisie shunted the eel pie to one side and sat down in a chair with a thump.

'Perhaps you had better explain.'

Hamilton did so, admitting how what had begun as an innocent flirtation had escalated into something beyond the control of either of them.

'I think a lot of Alice, Mama. I believe I love her.'

Maisie sighed.

'Alice is Alfie's betrothed. Did you never pause to consider that? Never think how hurtful this could be to him? Or the repercussions this could have on us all? And where, might I ask, does Emma fit into this equation?'

Numbly Hamilton listened as his mother began to extol Emma's virtues, reiterating her previous argument on how opportune it was to be joined in wedlock to someone like his cousin, brought up to the specific demands of the saddler's trade.

'Emma will make you a fine wife,' she told him. 'So you'd best put an end to this nonsense with Alice Courtney.'

'She'll be upset. I don't want that.'

'You don't have to be blunt about it. Try a gentle cooling off. Any girl will recognize the signs. And while you're about it you might step up your courtship of Emma. Show you love her. Cheer her up some.'

Hamilton said nothing. Avoid Alice? Make her feel rejected?

He only wished it were that simple.

★   ★   ★

Summer gave way to the gentler days of autumn. On every side the harvest fields lay bare under the misty blue of the late September skies. Barns and stackyards everywhere held fodder against the lean months of winter ahead. In the farming calendar it was a time of fulfilment and rejoicing, yet all Josh could feel was an aching sense of loss.

'Go seek her out, lad,' his father said. 'Put an end to that betrothal shenanigan an' bring her here where her belongs. Tes what you want, inna it?'

Sam Brookfield had long seen how things were and Josh gave his father credit for astuteness. He also knew, however, that what he suggested was out of the question.

'Father, I cannot. We're talking about a respected family here. Emma's name could be blighted for good and the scandal could bring discredit to Gideon Trigg's business. I cannot take the risk.'

'Aye, there is that. Well then, I dunno. Seems things will have to take their chance. If tes meant to be, then 'twill happen.'

Josh had his doubts, but he was in for a surprise.

The following Saturday — the first day of October — he went into town to the weekly market. He was leaving the square, his goods in a hessian sack on his back, when he heard a shout for help. It was a female voice and he shot a searching glance around. In a dark alleyway two drunken youths were attempting to rob someone of their money.

'Gi' us your purse! Gi' it here!'

'No, no! Get away from me!'

It was too dim to see properly, but though the victim appeared to be putting up a good line of resistance she was obviously no match for her attackers. Josh dropped his sack of purchases and sprang to the rescue.

'Ho there! You leave her be!'

His sudden appearance was unexpected and the attackers took instant fright and ran. On the grimy cobblestones a shopping basket lay overturned, its contents scattered. Josh scooped them up and replaced them before turning to the owner.

One look and he let out a gasp.

'Emma!'

'Josh? Oh, Josh!'

She flung herself into his arms, weeping and shaking in delayed shock. He held her close, stroking her loosened hair and murmuring endearments until the sobbing gradually abated and she grew calmer.

'Better?' he asked in concern.

'Yes.' She managed a wan smile. 'They must have been lying in wait. I was cutting through the alleyway and they jumped out at me. They'll be sorry, though. I gave their shins a kick or two. They'll sport a few bruises tomorrow.'

'It's glad I am to hear it,' Josh said.

He did not release her and she made no attempt to free herself. It felt right for her to be there in his embrace. For the moment that was all that mattered.

Josh knew then that he could not give her up. Whatever it took, whatever the outcome, he had to see her again. He had to explain how he felt about her.

He put her gently from him and spoke urgently.

'Emma. Will you ever forgive me for what I said? I was wrong to drive a wedge between us. Very wrong. Words cannot express how much I've regretted it. There's so much I want to say, but not here. Will you meet me tomorrow? Our usual time and place. Are you able to get away?'

'Yes,' she whispered. 'I'll be there. Of course I will. Josh, I've missed you so much.'

That sweet, drowned look in her eyes was too much to resist. He cupped her chin in his hand and pressed a kiss, very tenderly, upon her lips. Her arms sneaked around his neck and soon they were kissing as if neither of them wanted to stop.

People were passing the entrance and when, eventually, a housewife turned into the alleyway and came brushing past, they broke apart. Josh retrieved his sack of supplies and handed Emma her shopping basket.

'Come, I'll see you home. Tomorrow we'll talk.'

Together they walked through the town, turning off into Bridge Street and mounting the steep, uneven flight of steps to the Row where Gideon Trigg had his shop.

Outside the door they clasped hands briefly, and then Emma went inside. Josh threw a vigilant glance around. All seemed quiet. Locked in a daze of happiness and incredulity, he headed off for the inn where he had left his horse.

Someone had seen, however. Concealed behind a tall pillar, she watched the exchange between the two.

Once the path was clear she continued on her way, her neatly shod feet tap-tapping along the wooden boards of the Row, pet dog trotting alongside, a cloud of Attar of Roses lingering in her wake.

★ ★ ★

Alice was far from happy. Hamilton was avoiding her and she wanted to know why. She was really taken with Hamilton and had been certain he felt the same about her. So what was the reason behind the sudden cooling off?

'Suzette, my pet, it is not good enough,' she said to the dog, who gave a whine of response and looked for the titbit that was usually forthcoming.

'There.' Alice delivered the sweetmeat absently.

They were two of a kind, herself and Hamilton. She felt extraordinarily connected to him, relished his company. Some deep-rooted honesty within her accepted that Alfie — dear, constant Alfie — was too good for her and deserved better.

It was galling to think that Emma was still seeing her horse trader. Envy that her friend looked to be succeeding where she had seemingly failed churned her blood and a cold, hard shell of vengeance settled around her heart. She would bide her time to get even.

'For sure as nines it will come, my pet.'

She delivered a kiss to the soft fur of the dog's head and reached for the dish of sweetmeats. Violet creams, her best-liked. Hamilton had bought her them, and it would not be the last token of his affection.

She would see to that.

Later that evening she was letting Suzette out for a bedtime run in the rear garden that, along with others, flanked the sections of shops and dwelling houses, when she heard a faint noise from further along. A grassy lane skirted the properties, wide enough for access with a horse and trap.

The sound had come from the saddler's yard. Instantly alert, Alice let herself out of the garden gate and sped silently along until she reached the place in question. Someone was stealthily entering the stables.

She stood back in the shadows, eyes straining into the darkness, and after a few moments she saw the intruder leave the premises.

It was the tall, unmistakable figure of Josh Brookfield. What was he doing here? She had to find out. Breath held, she entered the yard through the rear gate and went into the stable where the two horses were bedded down for the night. It was hard to see in the gloom, but pinned to the wooden partition of the stalls was a crumpled envelope.

Alice snatched it up and made her retreat.

Back in her bedroom, she lit the lamp and saw that her find was directed to Emma. She ripped it open and scrutinised the scrawled missive that had obviously been written in haste.

Dearest Emma,
    Forgive me, but Father has taken a turn

for the worse and I cannot leave him.

I feel sure you will understand. Will be in touch. Trust me.
Ever yours,
Josh

So that was how the land lay. She might have known. Tempted to fling the letter into the fire that crackled in the small black-iron bedchamber grate, Alice resisted the urge. Perhaps the discovery could work in her favour at some point.

Eyes narrowed in thought, she folded the letter and stowed it securely away in her reticule.

She'd get Hamilton for herself yet. She would!

★   ★   ★

He wasn't coming.

Cygnus fidgeted restlessly as Emma peered with fading hope into the murk of the chilly October dawn, her ears strained for the telling beat of hooves. There was nothing. Nothing but the plop and drip of rain-sodden countryside and the dismal cawing of the rooks in the distant trees.

It wasn't like Josh to be late. Perhaps he had been unavoidably delayed. She would give it a little longer.

Overhead, rain clouds were again gathering and she shivered, pulling her cape more securely around her.

'Josh,' she said aloud. 'Where are you?'

The rain began. Lightly at first, growing heavier, and after a while Emma gave up and left. She arrived back drenched and miserable. Unsaddling, she automatically went through the routine of rubbing the horse down and giving him an armful of hay. Barney in the adjoining stall whickered to her, and as ever she fetched him some feed as well. Before she knew it she had buried her face in her old friend's mane and was sobbing quietly, whilst beyond the stable door the rain pelted down and the wind buffeted, shredding the trees in the back gardens of their crumbling canopy of leaves.

Once the storm of weeping had subsided, Emma mopped her cheeks with a sodden kerchief and headed for the kitchen.

'Look at you!' Maisie said. 'Soaked through. Best go and change before you take a chill. I have to wonder at the sense in young people nowadays . . . '

Her aunt's scolding followed Emma up the stairs and she reached her room with relief. She closed the door and stood a moment, conscious of something dark and formless having entered her soul.

He hadn't come. There had been a change of heart. He didn't love her after all. She was destined to stay here on Saddler's Row, year after year, growing old and out of temper like Aunt Maisie. Granfer Trigg was right — horse traders were a feckless lot.

Before divesting herself of her wet clothes, Emma snatched the silver bracelet from her wrist and dropped it into a vase on the mantel, where it lay among the lost hairpins, dust, and stray buttons of years, rejected and unwanted.

So much for lucky charms.

★   ★   ★

Plans went ahead for the betrothal. There was to be a modest celebration to which Alice, as Alfie's wife-to-be, and Alice's parents, were invited.

Maisie tried to get Emma interested in the preparations, but gave up in exasperation.

'You're looking proper peaky, Emma. Happen you need a dose of burdock.'

Emma submitted meekly to her aunt's ministrations whilst silently craving a remedy for a broken heart. For despite everything, she loved Josh still.

She knew she would never love anyone else

and it was harrowing that Hamilton had latterly become more attentive, showering her with small, ill-chosen gifts — ribbons of unbecoming brown sateen, gloves, a serviceable kerchief.

Emma stowed them sadly away and thought how more like a brother than a lover he was to her. How could she ever wed him?

The betrothal date drew relentlessly closer and Emma, in wilder moments that verged on hysteria, gained a certain relief from the fact that the wedding itself was some while off. Anything could happen in the meantime.

Something did. Something that was to change all their lives totally.

$$\star \quad \star \quad \star$$

'You've been avoiding me,' Alice said to Hamilton. 'Why?'

She had seen him crossing the street, undertaking a delivery with a set of riding harness over his shoulder, and waylaid him.

'Alice, please. Not now.'

'Oh, Hamilton.' She gave him a melting look. 'Can't you spare a moment for me?' Seeing that this had no effect, she hardened her approach. 'Tell me what's wrong.'

'Isn't it obvious? I'm shortly to be betrothed.'

'So? That never bothered you before. Don't you care for me anymore?'

'That isn't the point.'

'I'd say it was very much the point. Hamilton, my love, you and I are two of a kind. We both know what we want and neither of us is on the right path. Emma is no more for you than Alfie is for me.'

'Alice, she is to be my wife.' Hamilton faltered, and for one heart-stopping moment Alice thought she had won. He then said firmly, 'I must go. Goodbye, Alice.'

She watched him walk away from her, and a great rage welled up inside her. She wanted Hamilton for herself. It was her he loved. He would *not* wed Emma!

She whirled on her heel and set off smartly in the direction of the saddler's shop. Within minutes she was facing Gideon Trigg across the littered expanse of workbench, her colour heightened, eyes bright as a cat's.

'Master Trigg. There is something you should see.'

From her reticule she withdrew Josh Brookfield's letter and held it out. Frowning and silent, Gideon lowered the gleaming black leather bridle he was assembling to his bench, took the letter from her and scrutinised it thoroughly.

The atmosphere in the cluttered little

premises was charged with conflicting emotion. Opposite, Alfie sat watchful at his own bench.

Gideon raised his eyes from the sheet of paper that shook slightly in his hand, and regarded Alice under bushy brows.

'May I ask where this came from?'

'I saw Josh Brookfield leave it for her in your stable. It's been going on all summer. He and Emma are lovers.'

Alfie's stifled groan was loud in the silence.

'I don't believe it,' Gideon said.

Alice shrugged.

'Then ask her, sir.'

'Oh, have no fear, miss. I shall,' the saddler said heavily.

Emma quailed beneath her grandfather's glower. Never had she known him so angered, so unforgiving.

'I've given you a home, miss, and this is how you repay me! How dare you fly in the face of all you've been taught? Did you never spare a thought for your family's good name and reputation? Your aunt's feelings? Hamilton's?'

'Granfer, it isn't as you think.'

'What's this? So I'm a liar now, am I?'

'No! Of course not. I was trying to say — '

'Then hold your tongue and listen to me.'

She stood stony-faced and silent while he

raged on, her world as she knew it tumbling remorselessly around her. She longed for escape, but her grandfather's final words she never expected to hear.

'You can go, miss! Pack your things and leave. I never want to set eyes on you again. I've always feared things might come to this. Blood will out! Go on. Be off with you!'

She turned and fled, tears scalding her blind as she stumbled up the stairs to the bedchamber she could no longer lay claim to. Hardly knowing what she was doing, she dragged out a carpet bag from her tallboy and began randomly to fling garments into it.

A light touch on her shoulder made her look round into her aunt's troubled face.

'Emma dear, I've tried to talk to your granfer. It's useless. He won't listen.'

'I know.' She gave a shuddering sob. 'Aunt Maisie, I'm sorry.'

'Hush, child. What's done is done.'

'What Granfer accused me of was not true. Josh and I weren't . . . there was no misconduct between us. Granfer wouldn't say what was behind all this. He was too incensed to reason with. He wouldn't entertain anything I tried to tell him.'

'There was a letter. It was incriminating. He wouldn't show it to me. It has been destroyed. I don't think he knew what he was doing.'

'A letter?' Emma shook her head helplessly. 'I don't understand. Aunt Maisie, Granfer did say something puzzling — 'blood will out'. What could he mean?'

'Ah, Emma.'

A look of defeat crossed Maisie's drawn face. She sank down onto the bed, patting the space beside her.

'Come and sit here. Emma, what I'm about to say will come as a shock to you, but under the circumstances happen 'tis best that you know.'

Hesitantly at first, Maisie spoke of a secret she and her father had vowed would never come to light. Emma learned with dismay that the man she had called Papa was not her real papa at all. Her true sire was a midshipman who was betrothed to her mother and left her with child when he worked his ticket to the Americas.

'He didn't know about the baby — you. They were to be wed on his return from the voyage. 'Tis the old story, a storm at sea, the ship lost with all hands. Your mama was distraught.'

'And Papa? I mean . . . '

'My brother, Gideon, had always loved your mother. When he learned of her plight

94

he promised to bring you up as his own if she would wed him. Emma, it was a good union. They had you and then Alfie came along. They were happy in their marriage.'

'Alfie! He's not my true kin.'

Emma's thoughts rioted in miserable confusion. She could not take it all in.

'He is to all intents and purposes,' Maisie said.

An enraged bellow from downstairs brought them jumping to their feet. Maisie, wide-eyed in alarm, pressed a full purse into Emma's hand.

'Take this. 'Twill see you through until you can find work. Farewell, child. God keep you.'

In due course Emma found herself on the city street, being jostled by passers-by, the bulging carpet bag at her feet. In her hand she clutched the charm bracelet, retrieved at the last moment from the vase where she had abandoned it. Josh had given it to her. She could not leave it behind.

People were staring. Emma picked up the bulky item of luggage. Where should she go? There was only one place possible. Even if Josh no longer wanted her, perhaps Sam Brookfield would let her stay.

She set off purposefully, heading for the highway that would take her to Broxton, the Bickerton Hills and the horse trader's yard that had come to feel like home.

Fifteen long miles lay ahead of her. Tackling the journey on foot, laden with luggage that grew heavier with every step, proved very different from riding there. Before long Emma's boots had rubbed blisters on her heels, but she dared not stop. Already the short late-autumn day was losing some of its light and fear of the bands of brigands that roamed the hills spurred her on.

As she went, her aunt's recent words hammered on her mind. She had to wonder about the letter that had been so incriminating towards her. Who could have sent it? And why? It was so perplexing a matter that her head began to throb painfully and in the end she gave up on the quest and trudged dumbly on, growing more weary and dejected with every endless bend in the road.

Dusk was gathering as, tired and footsore, she hobbled stoically up the wheel-rutted track to the Brookfield Yard.

She knew from the lack of smoke from the chimney that all was not well. On reaching her destination, she discovered the yard gate swinging on its hinges, stables and cottage closed and shuttered — the occupants evidently gone.

4

Her heart thudding in alarm, Emma entered the stable yard and flung a look around her. There was all the appearance of recent abandonment. A wooden pail lay overturned beside the pump which dripped water, the sound magnified in the stillness of deepening dusk.

A coil of frayed and discarded rope draped the gatepost of the field where Hamilton had ridden Cygnus with a view to purchasing. It seemed a lifetime ago.

Reminded of that sun-filled day in June — smells of lush grass and clover, swallows swooping, a pair of deep-blue eyes smiling into hers — Emma gave a gulping sob. Where was Josh? Why had he deserted her like this? No word, not so much as a scribbled message to explain his absence.

On the heels of this came another thought. What of Josh's father?

Heedless of the pain in her blistered feet, Emma sped across the uneven cobblestones of the yard to the cottage. She tried the door, found it locked fast and moved on to the window. The shutters were closed and, lifting the solid wooden bar that secured them, she peered in. From what she could see in the dim evening light the room was unrecognisable — the furniture pushed aside, fire dead, all evidence of her old friend gone.

None of this made any sense at all. She looked at the deserted fields and wondered about Josh's future plans for the yard. What of the mare and foal he was contemplating keeping as foundation stock? What had happened to cause this apparent change of heart?

What should she do now?

Numb with shock and bewilderment, she stood mute in the desolate stable yard, whilst around her the darkness thickened and behind the hills a pale moon rose, gleaming between reeling clouds in the troubled autumn sky.

A single white owl wheeled ghostlike overhead with a piercing cry that jerked Emma out of her apathy. One for sorrow, she thought. Dear Lord, hadn't she sorrow enough?

In sudden desperation she searched the sky for a second bird, and was unashamedly relieved to see the female glide past on silent wings. Josh had spoken of the barn owls that roosted in the feed-loft above the stables. He believed that as long as the birds remained, the place was protected.

Sam Brookfield had smilingly said it was his Irish blood speaking.

As she watched the hunting owls it struck Emma how vulnerable she was, a woman alone and unarmed, easy target to any vagrant roaming the district. She saw the male bird swoop on some small, unsuspecting prey and return to its nest via the round owl hatch in the gable end of the building.

Maybe it was trying to tell her something. There, at least, she would find refuge for the night ahead.

First retrieving her carpet bag from the gateway where she had dropped it, she made for the shadowed stillness of the stables and climbed the flight of stone steps that ran alongside the outer wall, entering the loft and the heady sweetness of summer hay and straw. In a far corner, where she was less likely to disturb the nesting owls, she scooped together a deep pile of loosened fodder. Then, after removing her confining boots with a sigh of relief, Emma wrapped her cloak around her and lay down in the makeshift bed, closing her eyes determinedly against the dark, inhospitable outdoors.

Utter exhaustion washed over her. Emma's last thought before drifting off to sleep was the comforting maxim that things would be better in the morning.

Thin slivers of daylight slanting through the slats in the roof woke her. She lay a moment, wondering where she was.

Realization came all too swiftly. Swallowing hard, she sat slowly up in the prickly bed. The movement caused the purse of coins in the concealed pocket of her petticoat to brush against her with a heartening nudge, and her spirits lifted a little.

She was young, in good health and, thanks to Aunt Maisie, she had the means to survive, at least for a short while.

She took out the purse and counted the money. It totalled nearly six guineas — more than she dared hope for. She should have enough here to rent a room while she sought work. She would not think of the past. It was the future that mattered.

On that positive note she put the purse away and stood up, shaking straw bits from her skirts and hair. A few agonising moments were spent in easing her still-swollen feet into her boots. Then, collecting her luggage, she descended the ladder and went out into the cold grey light of dawn.

At the pump she swilled her hands and face and drank thirstily, conscious of a growling emptiness in her stomach. How long since she had last eaten?

Noon yesterday, her mind supplied. It had been a perfectly normal meal taken with Granfer Trigg and the family. Who would have thought her circumstances could have swung so disastrously in so short a time?

In her carpet bag was the package of food her aunt had hastily assembled for her. Emma pulled it out. The bread was stale, the cheese hardening, but she swallowed the meal down to the last crumb.

Feeling better, she left the yard without a backward glance, stepping out, her one thought to put as much distance as possible between herself and Chester.

She had reached the main highway to Nantwich, signposted 'Salter's Lane', when the clop of hooves alerted her to the presence of a fellow traveller. Alarmed, she threw a glance over her shoulder and was relieved to see the harmless figure of a carrier aboard his cart.

The man drew up beside her.

''Morning, missie. Tes early to be abroad. Can I offer you a lift? I'm bound for the township of Tarporley.'

Emma did not think twice. Her feet in her cramped boots were already throbbing painfully and Tarporley seemed as good a place as any to begin a new life. She tossed her carpet bag onto the back of the cart with the other packages, and clambered up beside the driver.

Chilly October air brushed her face as they clopped along. The carrier seemed glad of some company and kept up a lively chat that stopped her from brooding on her problems. He readily answered Emma's query about accommodation.

'The Swan's your best chance, missie. Tes a posting house, mind. 'Twill be noisy, what with the coaches arriving all hours and folks wanting food and a bed for the night. That said, the place has a sound reputation.'

They were passing some sort of industry to their left, an ugly scar on the gorse and heather clad hillside. A huddle of shacks surrounded what looked like a pit face, and there were yards with horses and laden carts and a great deal of noise and activity.

'What's that?' Emma asked, twisting in her seat to view the scene more thoroughly.

'Tes the Gallantry Bank Copper Mine,' the man replied.

She turned impulsively back to the driver.

'Wait! I'm looking for work. Could there be a vacancy there? I don't mind what it is. Cleaning, scribing, anything.'

Her mind worked feverishly. Chance was she would get lodgings nearby and thus be to hand should Josh return to the area . . .

The carrier was horrified.

'Forget it, lass. A young maid like you in that rough sorta place? You dunna know what you're asking.'

He whipped the horse to faster pace, effectively putting an end to Emma's thoughts in that direction.

Tarporley church clock was striking midday as they rumbled into the straw-and-dung-strewn courtyard of the Swan Inn. The hostelry stood off the high street, a three-storey brick building under a slate roof, its impressive canted bay windows testament to recent refurbishment of what was clearly a far older structure.

For a moment Emma's heart failed her. What would they make of her, a female travelling alone, young, with nothing to her name but the clothes she stood up in and a moderate amount of hand luggage?

The carrier was reaching for her carpet bag, and she had no choice but to disembark and take it from him. She fumbled in her cloak pocket for the few loose coins she kept there, but the man waved the gesture aside.

'Nay, missie. 'Twas my pleasure.'

He began sorting out his delivery and feeling herself dismissed, Emma steeled herself and entered the inn.

The foyer was oak-panelled and smelled of beeswax polish, damp wood from a fire burning sullenly in a stone hearth, and cooking from the nether regions of the building.

A young maidservant with straggles of mouse-brown hair escaping her frilled cap was flourishing a broom half-heartedly over the flagged floor.

Emma cleared her throat nervously.

'May I trouble you? I'd like to book a room.'

The girl looked up and Emma was disconcerted to see evidence of weeping in her reddened eyes and smudged cheeks.

'You're just in time, miss,' the girl said. 'The London stage is due. Us'll be burstin' at the seams then. Single, was it?'

'I beg your pardon?' Emma stared blankly. 'Oh, yes. A single room, please.'

''Twill be one-shilling-and-sixpence daily bed-and-board. Tes extra if you want a fire.'

The girl took a key from a numbered keyboard by the reception desk and gestured for Emma to follow. She was directed along a maze of creaking corridors and up a narrow flight of stairs, eventually coming to a stop outside a door displaying the figure seven.

It was a perfectly adequate room comprising a bed with blue counterpane, wash-stand with floral bowl and jug, tallboy and easy chair. A fire was laid in the brick fireplace.

'If you was wanting food, I could bring you something up,' the maidservant offered. 'Luncheon runs from noon till one an' supper's from six onwards, but we're flexible. Well, us has to be, what with the coaches coming in all hours.'

Emma considered the alternatives. A tray in her room was preferable to facing the unguarded stares of strangers.

'Thank you, I'll eat here.'

'Best I fetch it now,' the girl said. 'Us'll be rushed off our feet once the coach arrives. Will cold chicken followed by an egg custard wi' stewed plums be all right?'

'Yes, thank you. And a pot of tea, please. Do you have many staff here?'

The girl's look was bleak.

'Bless you, no. Just me an' Master and Mistress Cotterill. Oh, an' their lad, Roland.' She gave her mouth a downwards quirk, from which Emma made her own deductions. 'I'm Felicity, miss. Will you be wanting hot water to wash?'

The prospect of removing the dust and grime of the past twenty-four hours was a luxury not to be denied.

'Please,' Emma said eagerly.

The girl turned to leave, and as she did so

Emma's quick eye picked up the probable cause of her distress. She wore a drabbet smock over her ill-fitting gown of coarse homespun, but the loosened folds did not quite disguise the just-discernable high bulge of her belly.

There's always someone worse off than yourself!

Aunt Maisie's often-heard words chimed in Emma's mind, bringing a sad smile.

The distant tooting of a coaching horn had her moving to the window. Minutes later the London stage jostled into the courtyard amongst a great deal of shouting and barking of dogs. A stocky, bull-necked lad, no doubt the hapless Roland, sauntered up to take the sweating team of horses. A coachman in scarlet and gold livery clambered down from the high seat of the vehicle to organize the portable footstep, after which the passengers spilled out from inside the coach and from the top.

All at once the quiet of the inn was sliced by the trampling of feet, the slamming of doors and a strident female voice complaining bitterly about the discomfort of the journey.

Emma, rightly assuming her washing water and meal would now be delayed, went over to the bed, flopped down in its feathered softness and gave herself up to thought.

Chester. Was she missed? Or had her name

been banished from everyone's lips? Recalling her grandfather's unrelenting attitude, nothing would have surprised her.

⋆ ⋆ ⋆

'Leave it be, Maisie. The deed is done and cannot be undone,' Gideon Trigg said testily.

'But, Father — '

Irritation laced with something that could have been remorse crossed Gideon's haggard face. Maisie thought, with a shock and stab of concern for his health, for he was well past his prime, how her father had aged in the past twenty-four hours.

'I said enough!' Gideon answered, scowling. 'Lord bless us and save us, daughter, you'll drive me to distraction with that tongue of yours.'

Maisie drew a deep breath. It was not often she stood up to her father but in this instance she felt justified.

'It's not me that's the bother, Father. It's clear where the trouble really lies. Can't you see what this has done to us all? The boys in particular.'

'They'll get over it. Come to terms. That's life.'

'Alfie will not get over it. Emma is his sister.'

'Half-sister.' Gideon darted Maisie a fierce look under drawn brows. 'Let's get the details right.'

'Oh, for pity's sake! That's all in the past. You took those children on and brought them up as your own. Have you no feelings at all for Emma?'

'Aye. Bad ones.'

'That I find hard to believe.'

Maisie's voice softened. She reached out across the table and gently touched her father's clenched hand.

'Why not let bygones be bygones and fetch Emma back here where she belongs? Do it for me. I didn't have a wink's sleep last night for the worry of her. She's got no one in the world but us. Anything could have happened to her.'

'Enough!' Gideon brought his fist down on the tabletop with a resounding crack and stood up, the chair scraping on the quarry tiles of the floor.

He stormed out of the kitchen. There was a short pause as he reached for his greatcoat and hat. Seconds later the front door slammed with a noise that reverberated through the house.

Maisie found that she was shaking. Tears threatened, blurring her vision, and the familiar kitchen, with its pot-laden dresser and shelf of copper saucepans and jelly moulds, swam before her gaze.

'Mama? Are you all right?'

Hamilton had entered the room. He came to sit down in the chair his grandfather had just vacated.

Maisie gave him a watery smile.

'Yes, of course.'

'You and Granfer were arguing.'

'I don't need to tell you what about.'

'No. Mama, we cannot go on like this. We must look for Emma. We need to know that she's safe.'

'That's what I was trying to get over to your granfer. He wouldn't listen. He never does.' Maisie lifted her hands in a hopeless gesture and let them fall again to the table. 'He won't admit he's in the wrong. He always was hasty.'

'I fear he will have to live with his guilt. That's no easy matter.'

Hamilton's voice was loaded with meaning and Maisie's gaze sharpened.

'That sounds like experience speaking.'

He would not meet her eyes.

'In fact, Mama, I feel party to all this. If I hadn't allowed my eye to roam . . . '

'Hah, the glories of hindsight!' Maisie said wryly.

Hamilton looked up with a frown.

'Mama, please. I confess I still am taken with Alice. What I feel for her is altogether different from my feelings for Emma, but that does not mean I wanted rid of Emma and I certainly don't condone Granfer's action. Banishing her from the house! How could he?'

'Well, 'tis . . . complicated.'

Hamilton's eyes narrowed.

'There is more to this, isn't there?'

Maisie hesitated, and then gave a nod.

'There is. It was something your granfer alluded to in temper. Not very charitably, I might add.'

'What was it? Don't you think I have a right to know?'

Maisie's lips worked as she fought with indecision.

'I . . . oh, well, on my own head be it!' she blurted out at last. 'The fact is that Emma's parentage is not what's been put about. In brief, my brother Gideon was not her natural father. Emma's mother, Verity, had a previous understanding and ended up with child. My brother had always adored Verity. When he learned of her predicament he offered to wed her and give the child his name.'

Hamilton stared at his mother.

'So that's it! Granfer made his own conclusions. Like mother, like daughter, and

showed Emma the door. What balderdash.'
He broke off, allowing his thoughts to focus.
'What of the actual father?' he asked
curiously.

'He was a seaman. Apparently he and
Verity were betrothed. Verity never did
disclose his name, only that he sailed to the
Americas and his ship — the *Lady Grey* —
never made port. It was declared lost with all
hands.'

'Did he know about the infant?'

'No.'

Maisie drew a shuddering breath, stricken
at breaking a vow she had sworn to keep
— although now, if she were truthful, none of
that seemed to matter anymore. More crucial
was the damage the brutally delivered
revelation may have caused Emma.

'Emma's mother was from a good background. When my brother entered the scene,
her family did not take kindly to their
daughter marrying trade.'

'They cut her off? Just like that, after he'd
pledged to take on the child?'

'It is possible they were not aware of her
condition. In their eyes the union was a slight
on the family honour and not to be tolerated.
Your granfer set Gideon up with the saddler's
premises on the coast at Parkgate. He felt that
if the family saw that my brother was his own

man, independent of Chester and family obligation, it might resolve the problem. It didn't, of course.'

She heaved a sigh.

'Gideon was an accomplished saddler. It saddened your granfer to think that after apprenticing his son to go into partnership with him, it should then be denied him.'

'A sorry business,' Hamilton said thoughtfully.

'Indeed, though 'twas not all bad. Despite the troubled start Verity and Gideon made an excellent couple. Verity knuckled down to acquainting herself with the rules of keeping house and being a mother, and Gideon worked hard for his wife and family. He adored Emma from the moment she was born, and when Alfie came along his cup was full. It was a good marriage.'

'To end tragically with their death.'

'That is so.'

'And does Emma know all this?'

'I told her some of it. There was no time to go into details. Your granfer said 'blood will out', or words to that effect. Unfortunately, Emma picked up on it and asked me what he meant. So there you have it. Your granfer never did take to Verity. She was a glittering, vivacious creature. Not his type at all.'

'That's no reason why Emma should be punished.'

'No. When Gideon and Verity lost their lives and the children came here, your granfer and I made a pact never to reveal Emma's background. It seemed best at the time.'

'Yes, I can see that. Shall I tell Alfie?'

Maisie gave a small shrug.

'You may as well. It hardly matters now.' She leaned forward confidingly. 'I'd say your granfer is berating himself over his action. A slip of the tongue made in anger — and the past comes home to roost.'

'Emma must be found.' Hamilton stood up, resolute. 'Leave it with me, Mama. We shall see what can be done. And don't fret. Alfie and I will not breathe a word of this outside these four walls.'

She watched him walk from the room. He seemed taller, more positive — older even. It was as if the calamity that had befallen had somehow matured him. Maisie accepted that this was no bad thing, but what a disastrous turn of events to have brought it about.

★ ★ ★

Emma wasted no time in seeking employment. Despite the carousing downstairs that went on until the small hours and kept her

113

awake in the unfamiliar bed, she was up early the next morning. Breakfasting hurriedly, she went out to see what Tarporley had to offer in the way of work. Plainly dressed in a simple gown of dark blue woollen, her abundant hair tamed inside a bonnet unadorned by ribbon or flower, a cape around her shoulders, she considered her appearance appropriate for a working girl.

The sun shone briefly between the clouds; a beguiling, late-autumn sun.

Where should she try first? A shop? She could be a shop assistant, couldn't she? A housemaid? That brought a grimace. She would have to keep her carelessness in check, but if needs must . . .

She set off, pausing at a large dwelling calling itself, according to the iron-wrought lettering over an arched gateway, the Manor House. Its imposing, three-gabled grandeur seemed daunting and she moved on. Further along, a crocodile of children under the stern eye of a stiff figure in sombre brown was entering a low-roofed building set at the back of a churchyard. Could she see herself as a schoolma'am? Perhaps.

She continued into the small town. At a baker's shop she made her enquiries.

The baker's wife shook her head.

'Nay, dearie. My man and I run the

business between us. You might try the mantua-maker further along the street. They're always looking for girls to train up.'

Emma thanked the woman and left. Stitching was not her best-liked occupation, but she had to try.

'You have references?' the mantua-maker queried, her face tightening as a blush stained Emma's cheeks.

'Er . . . no,' Emma said. She had not given it a thought.

The woman brushed an imaginary speck from her impeccable skirt of black bombazine.

'I'm sorry. We have sufficient staff here.'

Emma lifted her chin and stalked out, pulling a ferocious face to herself as she did so. So much for a career in dressmaking!

The lack of character references, however, presented a problem. She would just have to see how things went.

She tried the haberdasher's, the milliner's, grocer's, a sweet shop, and even a wood yard in the likelihood of there being office work. None would take her on. Shop owners were genuinely not requiring staff or her sudden appearance, in a place where everyone knew everyone, hinted at caution.

★　★　★

After an entire morning's search, Emma returned to the Swan in a less optimistic frame of mind. What if she could not get any employment? How would she live?

Back in her room, she dropped the latch on the door and subsided into the easy chair. Absently she fingered the charms on her bracelet she had fastened on her wrist that morning, concealed beneath the cuff of her gown.

The delicate silver charms slipped familiarly through her fingers — church, wedding slipper, cottage, spinning wheel, cradle. The bracelet represented all the hopes and expectations of a young girl's dreams. What was it the stallholder had called it? A maiden's wish trinket, that was it.

Wear it always, Josh had said. *'Twill bring you luck.*

Not so far it hadn't, Emma thought, contemplating the sixth charm that was so reminiscent of the giver.

Tempted to wrench the bracelet from her wrist, she was alerted to the sound of harsh voices in the courtyard below. Frowning and curious, she went to the window to see what was happening.

The London stage had left and, to judge by the laden laundry basket at her feet, maid-of-all-work Felicity looked to have been in the process of dealing with the used bed linen.

She had been waylaid by the landlord. Bertram Cotterill's red-veined face was suffused with rage.

'Strumpet! Harlot! Breeding, inna you? How long did you reckon you could keep this from us?'

'Sir, please . . . ' Felicity wrung her hands in despair. 'I dinna know what to do. I've been out of my mind wi' worry.'

'An' so you should be. Workhouse brat! We took you on, me an' the missus. Gave you a roof over your miserable head, fed and clothed you, and this is how you reward us.'

'It wunna none of my fault. I was took advantage of. Ask him!'

Felicity jabbed a finger in the direction of Roland, who had emerged from the stables and was watching the scene with undisguised interest.

'Her's lying. 'Twunna none of my doing,' he told his father with a shrug.

From the doorway to the kitchen, Aggie Cotterill sprang to her boy's defence.

''Course it wunna. Accusing my lad like that. You're a wicked girl, and no mistake.'

'This is a respectable inn, miss. You can get out. Now,' the landlord went on savagely, spittle flying from his lips. 'You shall have a week's wages — and that's more'n you deserve.'

'But, sir, I have nowhere to go. Keep me on, I beg you. I'll work for nowt but my board . . . '

Felicity pleaded and wept, but her boss was unyielding. Soon afterwards, Emma watched the woebegone figure leave the inn, her bundle over her shoulder, whilst the landlord's wife looked frowningly on, arms folded over her ample chest.

After the girl had gone, Aggie Cotterill began berating her man, her complaints rising to where Emma stood at the open window.

'No servant anymore and me left with everything to see to! Tes more'n a body's capable of, husband. I've only got one pair of hands . . . '

Emma seized her chance. She hurried from the room, down the flight of stairs and along the maze of passageways and out. In the courtyard she presented herself between the sparring couple.

'Please, I couldn't help but overhear. If it's a maidservant you want, I'm looking for work. I can clean and cook and attend to the laundry. I can see to the horses too, if need be,' she added as an afterthought.

'Well . . . ' Bertram Cotterill rubbed his bearded chin in doubt.

His wife was more eager.

'Show me your hands, miss.'

Callused from riding and roughened with housework, Emma's hands had always been her bane, but never had she been more gratified at their contrast to Alice's dainty white specimens than now.

'Them's the mark of a working girl.' Aggie looked at her man. 'Husband, the Chester stage is due within the hour. There's bedding to change, rooms to prepare, fires to lay. I can't see to all that and the meals as well. What choice have we?'

The landlord knew when he was beaten.

'So be it. You shall have a month's trial, miss. Fetch your things and the wife'll show you your quarters.' His lips quirked in grim humour. 'You'll find it different from where you are currently. We shall see how you cope.'

'You will not be disappointed,' Emma said with quiet determination.

In her heart she felt sorry for Felicity, without doubt an innocent victim, but there was no getting away from the fact that one person's downfall often was another's gain.

Maybe there was something to be said for lucky charms after all.

★ ★ ★

Alfie rode into the saddler's stable yard and dismounted, patting Cygnus's hot and lathered neck. Church bells had been ringing when he left, but now the town lay in the grip of Sunday stillness. Since there was no sign of his aunt and grandfather, he assumed they had not yet arrived back from St Bridget's where the family worshipped.

Hamilton came out of the house to greet him.

'Well?'

'Nothing. I've enquired everywhere. No one had seen her.'

'Did you go to the Bickerton yard?'

'That was my first port of call. Hamilton, the place is deserted. The Brookfields must have moved on. I had a look around. Someone had slept in the hayloft. The straw was messed about and I found a footprint in the dust.'

'Emma's?'

'Could've been. Heaven knows what she thought when she found the place empty.'

Hamilton pressed his hand to his forehead. 'Dear God!'

'The point is, where did she go from there? It's been three weeks now, and still no sign of her. It's as if she has vanished off the face of the earth.'

They looked round as the tall gate to the

stable yard opened to admit Gideon Trigg and Maisie. Both faces showed the ravages of sleepless nights. Gideon's gaze went straight to the sweating horse and he scowled.

'Alfie, look at the state of that animal! Have you been racing him?'

'Sir, I thought he'd benefit from a gallop. He's been short of exercise lately.'

The scowl intensified.

'Best get him inside and rubbed down. And mind you throw a rug over him afterwards. Don't want the poor beast coming down with a chill.'

'No, sir.'

Gideon stomped off into the house, but Maisie held back. She pulled her warm woollen pelisse more closely about her against the raw November day.

'You've been out looking for Emma.'

It was not a question but a statement of fact and Alfie shrugged.

'I had to try, Aunt.'

'Of course you did.' She reached out to grip his hand. 'Did you have any success?'

'None whatsoever,' Alfie said.

Hamilton cleared his throat.

'I too have looked, Mama. It was my turn to make the deliveries this week, so I was able to combine the two. I found nothing. Either she's covered her tracks well or . . .'

He shook his head and Maisie gave a quick intake of breath.

'Don't even think it. I know there's been more trouble with the robber bands. It was in the newspaper. Your granfer read it out to me. I could tell he was concerned.'

'Where else could we try?' Alfie said. 'She's got to be somewhere. I've some errands to run tomorrow. I'll ask around. Mayhap I'll strike lucky.'

'Please God you do,' Maisie said softly, and giving them both a small smile she continued into the house, shutting the door gently behind her.

* * *

Emma had never been so exhausted. Up at five to attend to the fires, run off her feet all day long, rarely in bed before midnight. Days, weeks, merging into one. Life at Chester had been luxurious by comparison. Oddly, in some obtuse way she felt the change was justified.

Blood will out!

Granfer Trigg's words preyed on her mind. Now that she had fully digested it, the circumstances of her birth rankled. She was not who she had thought she was. She was the product of a union between two people unblessed by the vows of matrimony.

Never mind that her mama had wed the person she had called Papa, she was still that despised element of society. Emptying slops and scouring saucepans befitted a baseborn person like her.

One dark morning she was helping her mistress with the bread when the landlord entered the kitchen, bringing with him the chill of wind-driven winter rain.

'Ill news,' he said heavily, brushing raindrops from his face. 'A girl's been dragged from the river. Seems she were in the family way. No wedding band.'

Aggie's hands stilled over the dough she was pounding.

'Felicity?'

He shrugged.

'Happen.'

A choked sound of dismay escaped Emma's throat, quickly checked. On the whole she fared well with her employers. It was not her place to have opinions and she had no wish to jeopardize her position here.

'Let it be a lesson to others,' Aggie said tartly, though Emma had not missed the sorrow on her mistress's face.

Without another word they went back to working the dough. Pounding steadily, Emma let her mind wander.

Her acceptable terms with the Cotterill couple did not extend to the son Roland, whom Emma found too forward by far. The broad country voices, not easy on the ear at first, were now wholly acceptable to her. She tried not to dwell on the tragedy of the poor dead girl fished out of the river.

As always, her thoughts turned to home. What was happening there? She went on to consider the vexing question of the man who had sired her. Who had he been? Some wayward sailor boy, more in love with life on the high seas than the girl he had left behind?

What she was coming to realize was that everyone made mistakes. Everyone had their dark side. Her friend Alice had proved that.

⋆　⋆　⋆

The wind blew keenly across the Dee meadows and Alice, walking along beside Alfie, the pet dog trotting along at her heels, gave a shiver.

Alfie took her arm.

'Cold?'

'A little.'

In fact the shiver was due more to the conversation than any vagaries of the weather. As always the talk had turned to Emma, and Alice's conscience had stabbed.

Where was Emma? Had she found a safe haven somewhere? Or had she met her end? Another shiver took her and Alfie was all concern.

'You are chilled. Shall we turn back?'

'No, it's nothing,' she said absently. 'I was thinking about Emma. If only I hadn't — '

At once she realized her mistake and broke off, but Alfie was no fool.

'If only you hadn't . . . what?' He frowned. 'Alice, what did you mean? If your part in this sorry business has been misleading in any respect, perhaps you'd better say. Did Emma actually admit to you that she and Brookfield were lovers?'

'Well, not exactly. She . . . oh, Alfie, forgive me. What a foolish creature I am.' Alice gave her eyelashes a practised flutter but for once, Alfie was not to be wooed.

'Pray continue, Alice,' he told her softly, but with an undercurrent that alarmed her.

'I saw them together,' she burst out pettishly. 'They were talking and, and . . . '

'And you were jealous,' Alfie finished for her. 'I vow I can guess the rest. Come.'

He gripped her arm and began marching her back along the river path, the dog struggling to keep up on her stubby little legs.

'Alfie, wait. Where are we going?'

'Home,' he said shortly.

Without relinquishing his grip, he hustled her, protesting, up the flight of steps to the bridge and along the busy environs of Bridge Street, thence ascending the steep steps onto the Rows with the dog fortunately still in attendance.

Outside the front door of the vintner's, Alfie stopped.

'Farewell, Alice.'

The eyes that met hers were hard and accusing. Then he was gone, leaving her biting her lip in vexation at not guarding her words more carefully.

He'd be back, Alice told herself. He would miss her. As for Emma — she was a survivor. Emma would be all right. Of course she would.

* * *

A month later, Alfie still had not come round. Hamilton, too, had seemingly deserted her. Alice was devastated. She drooped around the house, snapped at her mother, rejected all attempts to cheer her. Even Suzette the dog failed to bring comfort.

In the end her father intervened.

'You are looking peaky, poppet. It's a fine day for a drive provided you wrap up warm, and I have one or two out-of-town clients to see. Would you come with me? I would be glad of your company.'

Put so gallantly, how could she refuse?

Bowling along in the carriage, the brisk wintry air whipping some colour into her cheeks, Alice's spirits rose. She knew she looked her best in her new winter travelling outfit of kingfisher wool braided with black.

'Where are we bound?' she asked her father.

'Tarporley,' he replied, plying the reins expertly as a phaeton approaching far too fast caused the horse to jink. 'I need to call at the Manor House. They give me regular custom. I've a mind to make them a gift of that new Madeira we have in stock.'

They were passing the Swan Inn and Alice was thinking what an attractive façade it had, when a figure in the courtyard gained her attention.

She was dressed in the working garb of a common maidservant, but the lithe shape and wayward corn-gold ringlets escaping from beneath the unflattering calico cap were unmistakable.

Alice blinked, unable to believe her eyes. It was Emma!

5

Emma applied the lighted taper to the kindling and sank back on her heels, willing the flames to lick and take hold in the massive stone grate of the hostelry foyer. Of all the fires she had to attend to, the first task of the day and by no means her favourite, this one was the most temperamental.

'Burn, can't you!' she muttered, flinching as a sappy twig spluttered and spat back as if in spite. Grimacing, she brushed a grimy hand across her forehead, leaving a smudge.

'Emmie? Where is the girl? Emmie?'

Aggie Cotterill's shrill voice carried from the kitchen and Emma looked up with a start.

'I'm coming, mistress.'

With a hasty clatter she gathered together the empty coal hod and battered wooden box of household tools and headed for the kitchen, depositing the box in the broom cupboard on the way. Behind her, the ugly old foyer clock began a strident chiming that sped her on her way.

In the flag-floored, low-raftered kitchen quarters that had doors giving off to pantries and storage lobbies, a blast of warmth met her, generated by a vast cooking range at one end and the crimson glee of an open fire five bars deep at the other. A cloud of smut-laden smoke gusted from the chimney of the latter — an ominous sign of the wind having changed direction overnight, heralding snow, if Bertram Cotterill's gloomy forecast was to be believed.

Aggie Cotterill stood at the range, wielding a big black-iron frying pan in which copious rashers of fat bacon sizzled temptingly, bringing a rush of juices to Emma's throat.

'There you are, Emmie,' Aggie said. 'Tes gone seven. The guests will be shouting for their breakfasts and they'll not linger. The coachman will be wanting to make tracks before the weather worsens, see if I'm not right.'

Deftly she transferred the bacon onto a large oval platter and indicated a stack of plates put to warm on a shelf above the hob.

'You can take this lot through to the dining hall for me. Dunna forget the bread. Look sharp, now.'

'Yes'm,' Emma said.

Her mistress's tone was commanding and leaving the coal hod next to the back door to be replenished later, Emma paused only to wash her chapped and smarting hands at the stone sink and did as she was bidden.

On the whole she found the travellers who stayed at the inn a genial crowd of people. She was developing a rapport that made her popular and won her the approval of her employers.

'Ah, here she be wi' the victuals!'

At the head of the long scrubbed table, the coachman rubbed his big red hands together with relish. A blunt-spoken man with a wind-buffed face and enormous side-whiskers, he gave Emma a smile.

'Any pickles, missie? There's nowt like a pickle or two to keep out the cold on a journey, especially when you're travelling up top.'

Emma, placing the laden tray down on the table, gave the man a nod.

'I'll fetch you some right away, sir. There's ale in the jug on the side table. If any of the ladies would like tea, I'll tell the mistress. Tea's twopence extra, I'm afraid.'

This last piece of information effectively stilled the eager looks from some of the female travellers, who resigned themselves to quenching the considerable thirst provoked by the salt bacon with the small ale provided.

Speeding back along the passageway on her errand, Emma came across the son of the house coming in from the stable yard.

'Roland, we need the coal hods filled for

the foyer and the dining hall,' she told him. 'And while you're about it you might replenish the kindling baskets. There was barely enough to start the fires this morning.'

'I'd give you a hand with the fires — for a small favour, like.'

A smirk lit Roland's face. He was an enormous, swaggering fellow with knowing boiled blue eyes and a bushy red beard and hair.

His very presence was intimidating, but Emma stood her ground.

'You'll get no favours from this quarter. Just keep your hands off me. I'm no Felicity, mind me?'

The smirk fled.

'I's sure I dunna know what you mean,' Roland said stiffly.

'Oh, I think you do. And while we're on the subject, you can forget any designs you may have towards the new girl when she comes.' Emma paused emphatically. They had become increasingly short-handed and Bertram Cotterill, after some garrulous chivvying from his wife, was taking on a second maid-of-all-work. Emma wondered if the girl had any idea of what she was up against coming here, and pressed her point home. 'Make no mistake, I shall be telling her what goes on here to unsuspecting female staff.'

Roland's face turned thunderous but Emma had already pushed past and failed to see the effect her words had had on him. Her employers she could tolerate but the skulking, over-indulged son she could not.

She knew it was a case of counting one's blessings. She had been kept on after her month's trial was up, was earning a moderate wage and had somewhere to lay her head at night. Yes, she had earned a scolding and a dock in money for breaking a meat platter, but then redeemed herself by concocting a balm for sore hands from goose fat and arrowroot, whilst inwardly lamenting the lack of base ingredients for the marigold salve that was Aunt Maisie's standard winter requisite at Saddler's Row.

All in all, she had much to be thankful for. Putting up with the son of the house was a small price to pay for that.

Her stomach growling, since she had been up before five and not a morsel of food had yet passed her lips, Emma fetched the crock of pickles and was relieved to see that Roland had gone on her return to the dining hall.

As a rule she breakfasted with her employers once the guests were fed. This morning they would doubtless have to wait until after their departure. The Chester stage was due at around ten. With the bed linen to change and rooms to prepare, breakfast this morning stood to be a woefully sketchy affair.

Here, Emma was wrong. When she went back to the kitchen she found that the new girl had arrived and the table was set for the two of them.

'Emmie, this is Prudence Twosey from the orphanage. She's to share your room. You may as well eat now, then you can show her what's what.'

Aggie Cotterill nodded towards the girl.

'Prudence, this is Emmie.'

'Mornin',' said the girl in a flat, nasal voice.

She was thin and sallow and seemed to have a permanent sniff. She did not look Emma in the face.

'Good day, Prudence.' Emma sat down next to her. 'Or do you like to be called Prue?'

Before the girl could reply Aggie Cotterill slammed down a plate of fat bacon and fried bread in front of Emma, her florid many-chinned face bristling in disapproval.

''Tes Prudence, if you please, miss. We had a Prue here once before. She were another who were no better than she oughta have been.'

Which Emma took to mean that there was another unfortunate victim of the son of the house.

'Prudence,' Aggie endorsed firmly. 'Like you're Emmie. We dunna want no highfalutin Emmas here.'

Emma swallowed a sigh. The only other one to ever have made light with her name was old Sam Brookfield. It had been done with playful affection and not designed to humble. The incident brought home to her, savagely, how low she had sunk within so short a space of time.

Breakfast consumed and the dirty pots dealt with, Emma took Prudence up to their shared bedroom under the eaves. With an east wind whistling through the cracks in the ill-fitting window and no fireplace, the room was punishingly cold.

'The bedcovers are worn thin. You'll need to sleep in as many clothes as possible,' Emma told the shivering girl. 'That is your uniform.'

She indicated the two gowns of coarse brown homespun, two starched white pinafores and ugly calico cap that lay on the second narrow iron-framed bed.

'You'll find a spare drabbet smock in the drawer. 'Twill help keep your clothes clean when you do the muckier jobs. All right?'

The girl nodded, sniffing.

'I shall leave you to unpack your bundle and get changed. Come down as soon as you can. We're busy today.' Emma made a wry face. 'Not that that's anything new.'

★ ★ ★

Much later, the long, hard day drawing to a close, the two weary girls sat before the kitchen fire, their hands cradling thick white cups of strong sweet tea and plates bearing wedges of plum cake balanced on their laps. Hard and ceaseless the work might be, but Emma had to hand it to the mistress, food was not stinted at the hostelry — when there was time to eat it.

She put her cold feet on the fender and as the warmth from the fire penetrated, the chilblains that always plagued her during the winter months began to pain and itch.

Aggie Cotterill came to sit with them, thumping her stout body down in the fireside rocking chair, her personal possession and woe betide anyone who requisitioned it. She looked the new girl over closely, her boot-button black eyes inquisitive.

'What's your story then, Prudence? Have you been at the orphanage long?'

'All my life, ma'am.' Prudence took a slurp of tea, savouring the strong sweet brew as if it were manna from heaven — which, for her, it probably was. 'I were left there on the front

135

step as a newborn. Seems I were wearing little knitted bootees. That's how I come to get my name, see. Twosey.'

Aggie nodded. A fictional surname was not unusual amongst orphanage incumbents.

'Emmie here were luckier. She knew her folks, dinna you, Emmie?'

'Yes, I did.'

In order to assuage her employer's insatiable curiosity, small confidences had been shared during the time she had been here. Emma had spoken briefly of her early years at Parkgate and how she had gone to live with relatives following the loss of both her parents. She had not given any details of her later life. For now, Chester and her banishment remained her own business.

She lifted her teacup to her lips and as she did so the firelight sparkled on the exposed charm bracelet on her wrist. Prudence's blank mud-brown gaze took on a momentary glimmer of interest.

'That's pretty. Were it your ma's?'

'No.' Emma put down her cup and saucer on the floor and carefully tucked the cuff of her gown back over the bracelet. 'It was a gift from someone I once knew.'

At that moment the back door opened to let in a blast of wintry air and the stocky figure of the landlord.

'Any tea in the pot?' he demanded, coming straight to the range to warm himself. 'Tes bitter out there. Too cold for snow, I'm thinking. Though on reflection, us did have a fall last Christmastide, remember, wife?'

'Aye, I do that.' Aggie heaved herself up out of her chair and went to pour him some tea. 'The roads were closed for over a week and folks here were stranded. Us nearly ran out of supplies. Tes to be hoped us dunna get a repeat this time. Happen I should have got in an extra bird or two, just in case.'

Emma, realizing with a start that tomorrow was Christmas Day, wilted under a sudden huge wave of desolation. It would be work as usual. There would be no festive good cheer this time, with Granfer Trigg carving the Christmas goose and Aunt Maisie bearing the pudding, alight with spicy flames.

What, she wondered, were they doing at Chester? Would her empty place be noted? Or was the seating reorganized around the dining table of polished mahogany in the front parlour, where this very special feast was taken, so that her absence was not obvious?

How was Alfie? If anyone at home was genuinely missing her, it would be her brother. Half-brother, reminded that small inner voice that cut her to the quick.

Had Alfie been let into the secret of her

begetting? Or was she now simply labelled as the black sheep of the family, a flibbertigib-bet, no longer worthy of thought?

★ ★ ★

Gideon knocked the dottle from his pipe into the blazing fire, coughing. Be damned to this chest of his; it was always worse come winter. Emma had concocted a linctus that had eased the problem considerably for him.

Emma. Her face swam up in his mind and he grew very still.

Across the hearth, Maisie was knitting a lacy shawl in soft blue wool, the click-click of her needles loud in the quiet of the room.

'Ah me!' she said suddenly into the silence. 'It seems wrong but I shan't be sorry when tomorrow's over. Christmas won't be the same without Emma.'

Gideon flung his daughter a wearied look.

'Don't start, lass. It won't do a scrap of good.'

'No, it won't. We'll just go round in circles, as always.' She heaved a sigh. 'These dark evenings get longer. Would you like a cup of tea?'

'I wouldn't say no.'

Gideon watched his daughter spear the needles into the ball of yarn and put aside her knitting. As she left the room, it seemed to Gideon that she looked more gaunt and angular than ever. He too had lost weight — he'd had to punch yet another couple of extra holes in his leather belt.

Sleep evaded him most nights. His temper was short. Guilt and remorse at his hasty action had become a constant ache. What had possessed him? Emma had brought light and laughter into the house with her sweet femininity, her generosity of spirit and that endearing tendency for chaotic accident that had been Maisie's bane but had privately made him smile. Of course her presence was missed.

His mind went back to a couple of evenings earlier. Alfie and Hamilton had finished for the day and gone through to the house, leaving him to extinguish the lamps in the work premises and lock up. He was about to turn the key in the outer door of the shop when he noticed a figure loitering on the Row outside.

It was Josh Brookfield.

Gideon realized he had been seen and he had no choice but to open the door and enquire what the young man wanted.

'I'd like to speak to Emma,' Brookfield said without hesitation.

About to shut the door in the fellow's face,

something in the young man's manner had given Gideon pause.

'Oh, you would, would you?' He spoke gruffly. 'And what makes you think she wants to speak to you?'

'Why should she not? Sir, may I be frank? I love Emma, and I was of the impression that my feelings were returned.'

'Oh aye? And as her guardian, can you explain why I was not informed of this development?'

'I do see how it must look and I offer my apologies. It was a recent declaration between us and goes back to the autumn, when our paths happened to cross again by chance. We . . . but I should try and explain. Sir, perhaps you were not aware that I assisted Emma with the young horse you had from me. It happened shortly after the transaction. He'd run off with Emma with the trap. She couldn't hold him. As luck had it I was in the vicinity and was able to help.'

'And events went from there? A whole summer of secret liaisons and I knew nothing?'

'Sir, nothing indelicate took place. You have my word on it. Emma had the makings of an excellent horsewoman and that in itself captured my interest. She was a ready pupil and I confess I looked forward to her company.

'Then, one day towards the end of the summer, she let slip of a betrothal between her and her cousin. I did the only honourable thing and put an end to the meetings. It was then I came to realize exactly how much Emma meant to me.' His voice faltered. He took a long breath to collect himself, and then looked Gideon straight in the eye.

'Master Trigg, I've written several times to her and not had any reply. I must know what's going on. I demand to be allowed to speak with Emma.'

Demand? No one demanded anything of Gideon Trigg! His temper, not helped by the strain he was under, had got the better of him. He'd sent the young man packing.

Now, Gideon was regretting the move. Brookfield travelled the length and breadth of the country with his work. If anyone had the means of tracing Emma, it was he. Gideon recalled, with a spasm of disquiet, the missives that had dropped through the letterbox along with the usual business mail. He'd torn them up, unread.

He gazed frowningly into the fire. Where could the lass be? What young Brookfield had said gave credence to what Emma had tried to tell him on that fateful day. Why in God's good name had he not listened, given her the benefit of the doubt, instead of jumping so disastrously to conclusions?

The door opened to admit Maisie with the tea tray, which she placed on the low table between them. Dealing with the tea, she sat down and gave him a searching look.

'Father, I have been thinking. Why don't we look for Emma?'

'What's this? Don't take me for a fool, Maisie. I'd lay a pound to a penny there's been a good bit of searching going on behind my back. All fruitless, I suspect.'

Maisie did not pursue that line of argument. She pursed her lips, seeking the right words.

'I don't know if you saw it, but in yesterday's newspaper there was a piece about an agency specialising in finding missing persons, and with every success, it appears. I've kept it by me. No, let me speak, please. Why don't we approach them over Emma? At least read what the article has to say, Father.'

Gideon directed his daughter a glower over his teacup. His lips worked as he wrestled with the matter. He decided to have none of it.

'Oh, have it your own way,' he heard himself say instead, in a voice choked with misgiving. 'Give the newspaper here. Let's see what it's all about.'

'What are you doing with that?'

Emma's voice was sharp and Prudence swung round guiltily, the charm bracelet dangling on her wrist.

'I . . . I were just trying it on, that's all.'

Emma advanced into the garret bedroom, for once oblivious to the icy draughts that ripped across the bare boards of the floor.

Christmas had come and gone in a frenetic whirl of activity. Throughout the whole of the festivities she had been lucky to snatch a few meagre hours' sleep per night. The New Year was now upon them and the Swan ran another full house. So exhausted was she that this morning she had overslept by a good thirty minutes. Prudence, never a willing riser, had taken advantage of the moment and also slept on. It had been a case of dressing hurriedly and running downstairs to attend to their duties.

Emma had been serving the noontide meal when she had realized that in her haste that morning she had left the bracelet by the bedroom wash-bowl. This had been the first opportunity to get up here and rescue it.

'Give it to me,' Emma said peremptorily, holding out her hand.

In miserable silence the girl unfastened the clasp and dropped the bracelet into Emma's palm.

'Dunna tell on me. I wunna meaning no harm.'

Not for one moment did Emma believe her.

'So you say. Just remember this. If I find you with any of my belongings again there'll be trouble. Now, you'd better get yourself downstairs and make a start on the dirty saucepans, or it's likely you'll be hearing the sharp edge of the mistress's tongue.'

Prudence flung her a look of pure dislike and fled, her booted feet clattering down the bare treads of the back stair.

Emma sank down on her bed and returned the bracelet to her wrist. In all her days she had never felt so dispirited, so at odds with life. Having to share a room with a potential thief was one burden too many.

Tears prickled her throat but she choked them down. Weeping solved nothing. She had quickly learned that. She rose and went to splash her face at the wash-bowl under the window. Ice filmed the surface of the water. Stoically, she broke it up, trying not to think of the plentiful supply of hot water so taken for granted at Chester.

She tidied her hair in the cracked and

spotted looking glass on the chest of drawers, pulled on her cap and left the room. The mistress would be looking for her downstairs.

'Ah, Emmie,' said Aggie Cotterill as Emma entered the kitchen. 'I've made a bite to eat for those two travellers we've had to put up over the stables. Take it across to them, will you? You'll need your shawl. Tes bitter out there.'

Emma had delivered the food and was heading back to the kitchen quarters when quite without warning her shoulders were grasped and she was swung roughly round. There was a snigger, a blast of ale-laden breath, and Emma looked up into Roland's triumphant face.

'Let go of me!' she gasped out, struggling.

His grip was vice-like and pulling her to him, he pressed his lips brutally to hers. She kicked and bit and tried to scratch him, all to no avail. The more she fought the more he persisted.

It took an unexpected shout from the outer doorway to the wine cellar to bring him to his senses.

'Emmie! My God, what's got into you, girl?'

It was the landlord. Having clearly misjudged the situation he came storming across to them, outrage in his flushed face and smouldering gaze. Roland's hands fell away and Emma, staggering, wiped her fist across her mouth in an effort to rid her senses of what had taken place.

'Sir. Believe me, I'm not to blame. I . . . I was molested.'

'Dunna you listen to her, Pa. She's like all her kind. A willing target.'

Roland gave Emma a sneer and went sauntering off, singing the opening bars of a bawdy song as he went.

Emma faced her boss defiantly.

'It's not true what he says. I didn't encourage him. I wouldn't. He's filth.'

'Dunna you speak of my lad like that.' Bertram Cotterill was incensed. 'I'd thought better of you, Emmie. Seems our Roland's right. You're no different from the others. I'm having none of this nonsense in my hostelry. You can pack your things and go!'

'Sir, please!' Emma wrung her hands beseechingly. 'It gets dark so early right now and it looks like snow. Where will I go?'

'You should have thought of that before you led my lad on. Tes to be hoped young Prudence has more sense. Now, get you out of my sight.'

Within the hour Emma was passing through the rear door of the Swan for the last time, the landlord's angry, unmerited words hammering on her brain. Aggie Cotterill, having developed a soft spot for Emma, had tried to intervene. But her man was resolute. She was to go immediately.

There had been nothing for it but to pack her carpet bag, bundle herself up against the cold in her cape and thick woollen shawl, and bid her mistress goodbye. She was acutely aware of Prudence's malicious gaze on her when, white-faced and quivering, she took her leave.

Snow flurried as she went through the wide gateway of the coaching yard. The sky was dark and lowering. All around, the landscape brooded under the prospect of bad weather to come.

Outside the gates Emma stopped, wondering what to do for the best.

She was back where she started, with no references and no prospects. It was midwinter. Not an ideal time for seeking work, though she had to try.

Where should she look? Tarporley itself she ruled out. News of her dismissal was sure to travel before her. Where else was there? At this point her wits deserted her. Her mind scratched and fretted hopelessly, trying to find a solution to what now felt an insurmountable dilemma.

It was no good. The sheer injustice of it all

was too much to cope with. She was not able to think anymore.

In the end she gave up trying and just stood there outside the heavy wooden gates of the inn, a slight figure, the snow settling upon her head and hunched shoulders, the carpet bag clutched in her chilled hand. Somewhere, a dog howled. The sound intensified and then faded away, and all that was left was the soughing of the wind, the sweep of icy flakes and the bitter, unforgiving breath of winter.

Taken by a surge of panic, Emma plunged mindlessly into the now whirling net of snow. Her feet carried her away from the little township and the security of cottage hearth and home, from which little beacons of light glimmered in the early afternoon dusk.

She made, instead, for the open country-side which was fast becoming alien and featureless under the snow-filled sky, and was quickly swallowed up by the gathering gloom of an approaching blizzard.

★   ★   ★

Alice stood at the window, gazing indifferently out at the wintry street. Her heart was sore. No Alfie any more. He had called, formally, to speak to her papa, telling him that the betrothal was ended for reasons 'that were not his prerogative to divulge.' Afterwards, Alfie had passed her in the hallway without as much as giving her a glance and the humiliating memory made Alice want to stamp a foot in vexation. There were, however, greater sorrows to bear. Worse, far worse, was the fact that Hamilton too was ignoring her and a small inner voice told her that she was not entirely blameless for any of it. What a shambles she had made of everything. How undeserved it was, when she had only been having an innocent flirtation. How was she to know how things would escalate? How with each passing day it would become plainer how deep her feelings actually ran for Hamilton Catchpole?

She was sure he felt the same over her. Why then the cold shoulder, the blatant refusal to acknowledge her if they happened to come across each other in the town?

The answer was all too obvious. Emma.

Perhaps, the thought occurred, if she were to make it known where Emma was, the act would help redeem her in Hamilton's opinion.

Then again, how to go about it without incriminating herself too deeply? She should have said something on that November day and not waited until now, bleak January and weeks after the event.

It was only then that it crossed Alice's mind to wonder how Emma actually fared. Through the shell of self-pity and boredom she had cast around herself, Alice felt a pinprick of remorse.

The young woman who had been her friend was reduced to skivvying in a tavern and she, Alice, had as good as put her there. She had not meant things to go so far and she frowned, thinking hard. Gideon Trigg was known to be a man of impulse and pride. By now he was sure to be regretting his reaction to the letter she had shown him — and he'd be finding it a hardship to admit being in the wrong. There would have been cautious searches made for Emma, more than likely prompted by Mistress Catchpole.

Some means of letting them know that Emma was safe and well, Alice felt, was all she needed . . .

She was jerked from her reverie by her mother, calling her from the hallway.

'I'm here, Mama. What is it?'

Her mother had come in from shopping. Despite her warm woollen pelisse and winter bonnet, she looked pinched with the cold.

'Alice, I clean forgot to call at the haberdasher on the market for those threads I needed. And didn't you want some embroidery silks? I really cannot face going out again today. Do be a dear and get them for me.'

About to refuse, Alice thought twice. It was true, she was short of silks for the sampler she was working on. Also, was it not standard practice for Gideon Trigg to stock up on harness buckles and other saddler's accoutrements from the brass-smith's stall?

She just might bump into Hamilton on his way to collect the goods, in which case she had best put on her new cherry-red cape with the fur-trimmed hood and muff — so becoming, her looking glass told her.

Snow was again falling as she stepped smartly into the market place, her pet dog under her arm. She had forgotten it was the beast sale as well as the usual trade stalls and trod her way carefully between the piles of soiled straw and dung that littered the cobblestones with their covering of dirty ice-packed snow.

All at once she stopped in her tracks, her eyes widening. For there ahead, tying a couple of horses to a tethering post, was Josh Brookfield.

Was this the opportunity she sought? Perhaps here was her go-between, the one to brighten her name without giving away too much disquieting detail.

She drew a resolute breath and went to speak with him.

'Master Brookfield? Good day, sir. You may not know me. I'm Alice Courtney — Emma's friend.'

He looked at her with that penetrating blue gaze, the lines of his face set and wary. My, what a handsome fellow he was, to be sure. Alice summoned her most winning smile.

'Sir, forgive my boldness but I was in Emma's confidence.'

'Was?'

He picked up on that one word and Alice, realizing that she was dealing with no fool, spoke with care.

'Well, yes. There was a . . . a misunderstanding. Master Trigg found out about you and Emma.' She glossed over the finer points, adding a little fabrication so as not to show herself in too bad a light. 'Emma is no longer at Saddler's Row. She was cast out.'

'Banished?' He stared, plainly stricken. 'Why so?'

'Master Trigg wouldn't tolerate what happened and told her to leave his roof.'

'Just like that? For pity's sake! There was no wrongdoing between us.'

'Try telling Emma's grandfather that. Oh, I dare say by now he's mortified over what he did, though it's clearly a little late for self-recrimination. The fact remains that Emma has vanished without trace. If they could only know that she is well and thriving, it would help put their minds at rest.'

The man was frowning and silent.

'Why are you telling me this?' he asked at last.

'Because I know where she is,' Alice replied succinctly.

★　★　★

Never had Josh made a sale with such recklessness. With the coins from the transaction jingling in his money pouch, he mounted his horse and set off through driving snow and hail, heading at a gallop for the Tarporley turnpike.

Emma. Emma. Emma . . . The thundering hoofbeats spoke her name, were rhythm to his pounding thoughts. He had tried to contact her, had no response, gone in desperation to the shop and questioned Gideon Trigg. Again he had drawn a blank.

That night he had not known what to think. He had stood in the street below, looking up at the building for sight of her, and all the while she had not been there. Banished, and by the very one responsible for her welfare. What had come over the man to have acted so irrationally? Small wonder the saddler had looked so wretched.

The weather was worsening and Josh checked the horse accordingly. The battering wind seized his breath and continued to unleash its burden of icy droplets, stinging his face and all but blinding him. Would he ever get there?

His comfortable lodgings at Flookersbrook came to his mind, shamefully, and were dismissed. All the comfort in the world was worth the sacrifice for Emma.

At last, snow crusting the horse's mane and the rider's shoulders, hands frozen on the reins, Josh caught the welcome whiff of woodsmoke from distant chimneys, saw the glimmer of lamplight through the swirling whiteness, and minutes later he was trotting thankfully into the yard of the Swan Inn, the horse lathered and steaming.

A lad peered out from the doorway to the stables. Josh, dismounting stiffly, called across to him.

'Here, fellow. Take my horse and rub him down well. See that he has a warm mash. Is the landlord about?'

'Aye. You'll find him inside.'

The lad came unwillingly up, a sack over his head against the weather. He took the

154

horse and Josh, tossing him a coin, strode into the inn and pounded on the desk for attention. After a few moments a girl in an ill-fitting gown and floppy calico cap appeared.

'Sir? Can I help?'

'A hot posset wouldn't come amiss. First, I want to speak to Emma Trigg.'

'Emmie?' The girl looked at him with a frown. 'You're too late, sir. Emmie's gone.'

Josh stared at her in disbelief.

'Gone where? Home, to her grandfather's at the saddler's shop at Chester?'

'I dunna know about a saddler's shop. Her's been turned off.' The girl spoke with relish. 'For misbehaviour. The landlord dunna allow any of that here.'

Josh's expression darkened.

'Misbehaviour? Emma? Poppycock! If there's been any wrongdoing the blame does not lie with her. So tell me. Where has she gone?'

The girl lifted a shoulder in a shrug.

'That's anybody's guess. She were on foot. Tes a wonder you dinna pass her on the road.'

'What?' Josh could not take in what he was hearing. 'She left today? In this?'

An infuriated gesture indicated the conditions beyond the window. The wind moaned in the chimney, sending down a splattering of hailstones to fizzle blackly on the hearthstone.

'God save us, doesn't anybody have an ounce of common decency or compassion anymore? No, I saw nobody on the road. It was impossible to see anything in the blizzard I've come through. It's to be hoped Emma's taken shelter somewhere. Otherwise I'll not vouch for her chances!'

The girl blinked, as if the enormity of what had happened had only now occurred to her.

'Will I get you that hot posset, sir, and mebbe something to eat?' she enquired timidly.

'What? Aye. I'll travel the better with food inside me. But be quick about it.'

He would give it an hour. That should see the horse rested for the journey back. God willing, he'd come across Emma on the road. Failing that, someone would surely have news of a solitary female traveller, wouldn't they?

★ ★ ★

Emma, battling through shrieking wind and stinging sheets of sleety snow, had made her retreat as far as the Whitchurch turnpike. Disorientated in the face of the blizzard, and weakening, she inadvertently strayed off the road and went a little way before realizing her mistake. Gasping and slithering on the glassy surface, she found herself on a rough uphill track that was fast disappearing under a thick coverlet of snow.

Fear clutched at her. She had to get back to the main highway. Now, before she lost her bearings entirely.

She stood a moment, her carpet bag clutched to her, the wind tearing at her hair and skirts, and peered feverishly into the whipping swirl of flakes.

Taking a chance, she set off in what she hoped was the right direction.

It all happened suddenly. She missed her footing and pitched headlong, rolling over and over down a steep and bumpy hillside. Her carpet bag lost, she grappled frantically in the snowy ground to try and arrest her fall, but it was hopeless. She reached the edge of what was actually a deep gorge and went hurtling over the side.

'He . . . ee . . . elp!' she screamed as she fell, weightless, through billows of icy snow, her voice torn away by the violent eddies of air that buffeted the slopes.

She came to a stop with a thump that knocked her senseless, the fall broken by a spindly rowan sprouting between the rocks. She lay motionless, the snow happing up around her, covering her tracks, and was unaware that at that moment Josh was riding past on the top road with hope in his heart for sight of her.

6

The distant lamps of Chester were casting a yellow glow into the evening darkness when Josh rode into the stable yard at his Flookersbrook lodgings on the outskirts of the city. He flung himself wearily from the saddle and led the horse stamping and snorting into his stall, their breath and the lathered flanks of the animal steaming in the bitter air.

'No luck again today, Diamond,' he said to the horse. Unsaddling, Josh scooped up a fistful of clean bedding straw, twisted it into a wisp and began to work his mount over.

His mind was troubled. This was the second day of searching for Emma, another fruitless day of sifting through silent, featureless countryside locked in the punishing grip of winter. Alehouse, farmstead, humble cottage; no matter where he had enquired, heads had shaken depressingly. Unspoken on many lips were the words none ventured to voice aloud.

A young woman alone, travelling on foot in the worst blizzard in living memory? Good grief, she stood not a chance of survival!

'She's here, somewhere. I just know it.'

Josh's vehement tones echoed and boomed into the high rafters of the building, and the big black horse turned his head enquiringly, before moving pointedly forward to inspect the empty manger.

'Patience, lad. I'll fetch your feed. An extra measure, methinks. It's been a long day.'

Having dealt with the horse, Josh went into the lodging house to the welcoming ambience of good cooking smells, blazing log fires and lively conversation and laughter.

The harassed red face of his landlady appeared round the door to the kitchen quarters.

'So there you are, sir. Supper's served. Go through and sit you down. Tes beefsteak and kidney pie tonight, with a nice plum duff and sweet custard sauce to follow. Good thing I've made plenty. I'd given you up for lost.'

'And lose out on Mistress Bradely's supper? Never!'

Josh flashed her a smile and went to the dining hall to join the other travellers at the supper table. The piping hot, savoury-smelling dish that was placed before him was welcome and lifted his spirits somewhat. He ate quickly and abstractedly, his mind busy, and by the end of the meal he had reached a decision.

Come Thursday he had to be at Shrewsbury for the horse sale. Before he left he would seek out Emma's friend, Alice Courtney, and tell her what had transpired. He might be pushing his luck, but perhaps she could throw some light on where Emma might be.

★   ★   ★

Chilly air stung his nostrils as Josh rode across the Dee Bridge, his saddlebags packed for the journey ahead. Here within Chester's protecting city walls the snowfall had been lighter. What remained was churned by the constant trampling of hooves and the passage of wheels, reducing the roads and byways to a slushy mire puddled with icy water that was hard on the horses and hazardous to unguarded pedestrians.

Josh recollected having seen the young Courtney miss, a coquette if ever there was one, giving her pet dog an early walk in Grosvenor Park, though whether she would feel fit to risk her dainty footwear in the present conditions was debatable.

Here he had misjudged Alice, for the striking figure in cherry-red and small fluff of a dog coming towards him were unmistakable.

161

He dismounted, raising his hat.

'Miss Alice. What a sight for sore eyes. Good morrow to you. May I steal a moment of your time?'

Pretty words generally worked with good effect. Josh was gratified to see the startled face take on a simper of pleasure.

'Why, Master Brookfield. Charmed, I'm sure.' She hesitated, apprehensive. 'Is there news of Emma?'

'Aye, though not good, I fear. I went to the Tarporley hostelry. She'd just left their employ. I must have missed her by a hair's breadth.'

'Oh.' Alice bit her lip. 'Did they say where she'd gone?'

'No. Seems she was turned off.'

Tersely, Josh revealed what he had learned. Alice gave a snort of disbelief.

'Emma? Flirting with the innkeeper's son? Phooey!'

'Those were my feelings exactly, and I told the landlord so. The weather at the time wasn't fit to turn a dog out in, let alone a young woman weighed down with luggage. The point is, where has she got to? I've searched every inch of the Whitchurch turnpike and found no trace. It's thought she perished in the blizzard and lies hidden in a drift somewhere. In no way do I go along with that,' he added at the young woman's strangled gasp of dismay. 'Miss Alice — '

'Please. It's Alice.'

'Alice. May I be frank? I have come to love Emma dearly. I shall go to any lengths to find her. Tell me, have you any idea at all of where she may have fled to?'

Her face puckered in thought.

'Could she have strayed off the road in the snowstorm by mistake? Mayhap she saw a light at a window and made for that. Did you try any of the lanes off the turnpike?'

'Lass, have you any notion of how it is out there? Drifts like castles and just as impenetrable. I'd defy anyone to get through them.'

A brewery horse and dray lumbered close by, the driver cracking his whip, the heavy wheels splattering filthy snowmelt in all directions. Black Diamond shied skittishly, causing Josh to break off to quieten the animal.

He then turned again to Alice.

'I have business matters that will keep me away for several days, but I shall return as soon as possible. Should you hear anything of Emma in the meantime, could you leave word at my lodgings? It's Mistress Bradely at Flookersbrook.'

'Well, yes, but, sir, I don't understand. Why

lodgings? What of your Broxton yard?'

''Twas Bickerton, up in the hills. I gave it up. What with Father passing on and other things, it seemed best. The lease was due to expire anyway.'

'So your papa is gone? I'm sorry to hear that. Please accept my condolences. Emma always spoke fondly of him. She wouldn't have known.'

'I'm not sure. I wrote to her several times, explaining the situation, but whether she received my letters is anybody's guess. It was all so sudden — meeting up with Emma again, Father dying . . . I wasn't thinking straight. Besides, the yard had its drawbacks. This trouble with parties of marauders worsens. There's no telling what they might get up to next. It was not a place I would have taken a wife to with an easy conscience.'

Alice's eyes widened in surprise.

'You were planning to wed?'

'Yes. I had a notion of getting some cash together quickly so as to secure premises more suited to a family man.'

A neat little house somewhere, with a stillroom facility and a few rod of ground for Emma to grow her physic and kitchen herbs, and yards, stabling and a tidy acreage of land for him to conduct his business. He could picture the very thing.

'There was a sale up north where I knew I'd get a good price for my stock. I needed to get up there right away and left Emma a note telling her to wait for me. Better if I'd tried to see her and explained, but there it is.' He drew a shuddering breath. 'Alice, I can't imagine life without Emma. I must find her.'

Desperation rang in Josh's voice. He glanced away, momentarily overcome, and did not see the flash of envy and longing his words had provoked in the listener.

Mastering his emotions, Josh straightened.

'I must go. There's no telling what the roads will be like between here and Shrewsbury. You will do as I ask?'

'I will. Safe journey, sir.'

Alice stood back as he mounted up, the dog clutched safely to her while the horse twirled and jinked at the prospect of a journey.

A nod of farewell, and Josh dug his heels into the stallion's sides and sent him plunging away, clots of sludgy snow spattering out from beneath the clattering hooves.

★   ★   ★

Alice watched him go, resisting the urge to stamp a well-booted foot in a mixture of pique and crushing disappointment.

Dear goodness, wasn't it just her luck to have her plans thwarted? At this rate she would never win back Hamilton's favour.

She put the dog down and, mulling over what Josh had told her, continued into the deserted park where the park-keepers had been busy clearing the walkways of snow, the dog trotting obediently alongside. Alice took her usual route between winter-bare flower-beds towards a deserted bandstand, and as she went a trickle of unwelcome speculation entered her mind, stirring a cold dread within her.

If it was true that Emma had succumbed to the horrendous conditions then she, Alice, was instrumental in bringing that about. She had as good as taken the life of her one-time dearest friend and ally — loyal, trusting Emma. How could that be? She hadn't meant things to go so far!

Deception had played a part, too. She had led Josh into believing that her friendship with Emma held fast, when this was not strictly the case.

Alice walked on, grappling with an increasing sense of panic born of guilt and remorse.

Why had she not spoken up sooner? Even allowing for Gideon Trigg's intractability, a degree of searching must have gone on for Emma, though done behind the saddler's back. Why had she not sought Hamilton out and pointed him — discreetly, of course — in the right direction?

Emma's face as she had last seen it, flushed with eager anticipation at seeing her handsome horse trader once more, appeared before her mind's eye. It touched some hitherto untapped region in Alice's heart, and shame rippled through her.

Swallowing hard, she strove for logic and reassurance. Emma was no fool. She would surely have sought refuge from the blizzard, wouldn't she?

'That's it, Suzette, my pet,' she murmured to the dog. 'Please God that Josh Brookfield is right and Emma is still with us. We must be alert for word of her.'

The horse trader's revelations had been illuminating, and Alice felt suddenly very much alone. How glorious to be so cherished, so desired. Would anyone ever love her like that?

After all, one good turn was said to deserve another. She must put her faith in Cupid and trust that they were on the right track. Then, with Emma safely wed to her true love, Hamilton's way would be clear for her.

Moderately cheered, Alice reached the park

exit and headed off for home and a warming cup of hot chocolate.

★ ★ ★

'Mama, it's about Alice. I know now that I love her. These long days and weeks of estrangement have made me realize exactly how much. I must see her again.'

Hamilton was decisive and Maisie sighed. She had feared it might come to this.

'Well, you know my feelings on the matter. All I can do is repeat what I've said before. Alice Courtney has her faults.'

'Haven't we all?'

'Indeed, though it hinges on to what degree. Alice strikes me as being self-obsessed and conniving. She's a meddler. She got her hooks into Alfie and now she's doing the same with you. It wouldn't surprise me if she knew more about this unfortunate business with Emma than she cares to divulge.'

'Never!'

Maisie rolled her eyes helplessly.

''Sakes, don't they always say love is blind? Think about it, Hamilton. She and Emma were friends. Young girls exchange confidences. It stands to reason that Alice will know more about what went on than any of us.'

168

'You believe she knows where Emma might be?'

'That I cannot say. Possibly not.'

'I value your opinion, Mama. In fact . . . ' Hamilton broke off, frowning and troubled. 'There was something Alfie let slip. It was after he had ended the betrothal. I don't recall the actual words but it alluded to Alice having played a part in Emma's fall from grace. He wouldn't say more — you know how close he is. He'll not run anyone down, either, not if he can help it. But something dire must have happened to make him finish with Alice.'

Hamilton drew a breath.

'Mama, my mind is made up. I shall go to Alice and find out what she knows. Though I warn you, whatever is revealed, it won't alter my feelings for her.'

He made to leave, but Maisie stayed him with her hand.

'One moment. I want to tell you what has been decided with regard to Emma. A private investigator, one Sylvester Rudge, has opened up an office on Watergate Row. Your granfer has made us an appointment to see him.'

Hamilton blinked in shock.

'Granfer has? That's a change of heart.'

'Oh, he's not as unrelenting as he makes out. This business with Emma has affected him sorely. Let us hope that Master Rudge is able to trace Emma.'

'And bring her home?'

'If God so wills,' Maisie replied with a wan smile.

★ ★ ★

Sylvester Rudge was a big, shambling man of middle years, with perpetually untidy grey-brown hair and a disarming smile that hid an exceptionally shrewd mind.

He used this smile now to woo Mistress Catchpole out of the worried fretting that made her pluck unwittingly at a loose thread on her cape, and visibly relax.

In the dingy little office on the Watergate, a small fire of sea coals glowed in the grate. The air was redolent of dust, of paper and ink and a trace of pipe tobacco from a previous occupant.

Rudge studied the face on the miniature his clients had brought with them.

'An attractive young woman, I warrant. May I hold on to this for now? It could help with my enquiries.'

'By all means,' Mistress Catchpole said. 'It is a recent likeness. We had it done last year for Emma's twentieth birthday.'

'Does she feature her mama?'

'A little. Perhaps more in manner than face.'

'Like her papa, then.'

'Well . . . ' The woman squirmed uneasily in the straight-backed chair, darting her father a cautious look.

Gideon Trigg cleared his throat.

'You may as well know the whole of it, Rudge. There's a history here. Emma's mama came from a well-set-up family. Her papa was a seafarer. The fellow got Verity in the family way and made off.'

'To be fair, he didn't know of Emma's mother's condition,' Mistress Catchpole put in hastily. 'Verity assured us of that.'

'Ah. The lady's full name at the time?'

'Verity Amelia Dawne.'

Rudge looked up in surprise from where he sat at his desk, quill poised.

'Would that be the Dawnes of Mollington? A very prestigious lineage.'

'Indeed. They did not wish their name to be besmirched by the daughter's fall from grace.' The woman's tone was wry.

Rudge wrote ponderously in his book, the scratch-scratch of the quill loud in the silence.

'There. I think I have all the details. You believe there was an assignation in progress between the missing girl and the horse trader Josh Brookfield.

'The girl left your roof nearly four months ago in October last year. You suspect she made for the Brookfield yard at Broxton in the Bickerton Hills, though according to your son's and nephew's findings, the yard is now abandoned.'

'That is correct.'

'Master Trigg.' Rudge directed the saddler a piercing look. 'You say young Brookfield approached you recently. Did he give any indication at all as to why he had vacated the premises?'

'No. He spoke only of Emma. Seems he weren't aware she were no longer with us.' Gideon Trigg made a helpless gesture with his hand. 'I should have questioned him further. Would that I could go back and start again.'

It was the eternal plea of the desperate. Rudge let a small silence hang before continuing.

'This friend of Miss Emma's.' He consulted his list of names. 'Alice Courtney. 'Twas she brought your attention to the letter that started everything off. Would an interview with her be possible?'

'That would be out of the question,' Mistress Catchpole replied. 'Her papa would never allow it.'

Rudge struck a line resignedly through the

name and leaned back in his chair, mulling over his next move. Overnight the wind had changed and sleet now slithered down the grimy window. It would be an uncomfortable ride up into the hills on the morrow.

'That, I think, will be all for now. With your agreement I shall go to the yard and see what I can discover. May I call on you on the way back, or do you prefer to wait and see me here?'

The woman drew a quick intake of breath.

'Come to the house, do. We shall be anxious for your news.'

'Very well, madam.'

Rudge gave her the full force of his smile. This was an interesting case, promising many twists and turns. He liked these people. He would do his best for them.

Then again, he always did.

* * *

The sleet had ceased next morning, but the leaden sky hinted of a return to snow when Rudge followed the steep road to the horse trader's yard, the collar of his greatcoat turned up against the bitter wind that gusted, his sturdy roan gelding picking a way stoically through the tracts of packed ice and snow that lay thickly here.

As expected, the yard was deserted. Inspection of the feed loft above the stables revealed signs of someone having slept up there.

Rudge's trained eye detected a flicker of white in the dimness. It was a lady's kerchief, embroidered with the initials EVT. Emma Verity Trigg. So she had been here, but what happened next?

Some instinct told him she had not fallen foul of the ruffians that roamed the hills.

His mind busy, Rudge returned outside and threw a look around at the well-kept buildings and yards and snug cottage. What would make a young horse trader with an ailing sire want to leave so ideal a place as this?

The answer was immediate. A bereavement. He had passed a church on the way here. It would do no harm to investigate the churchyard while he was here.

At Holy Trinity, Bickerton, the churchyard within its tall protecting yews yielded the information he sought. Just inside the lychgate a carved memorial of locally quarried sandstone announced that Kathleen Mary, beloved wife of Samuel Thomas Brookfield, lay here.

Rudge ran his eye over the inscription.

Kathleen Mary of Donegal, Ireland
Who departed this life 10th June 1820
Aged 26 years
'Not gone from memory,
not gone from love'

A more recent interment proved Rudge's hunch gratifyingly correct.

Also husband of the above
Samuel Joshua Brookfield of Bickerton
Who departed this life 7th October 1850
Aged 73 years
'Together again'

The poignant simplicity of the epitaph brought a lump to Rudge's throat. It was sudden and unexpected. He had thought to be hardened to life's miseries by now.

Rudge gazed at the headstone, thoughtful. So Sam Brookfield had met his end in the autumn of last year, after which the son had sold up and gone. And Emma, finding the place abandoned, had fled — perhaps hoping to find her lover? But in which direction would she go? Had she some inkling of where he might be, or was it a random guess?

Leaving that quiet place, Rudge pondered on his next move. A mile or so further on was the Gallantry Bank Copper Mine. Happen an enquiry there might not come amiss.

Reaching the premises, Rudge located the office amongst the collection of wooden shacks surrounding the mine face. Here he questioned the clerk of works, producing the miniature from the inner pocket of his greatcoat.

The fellow took the item with ink-stained fingers, twisting it this way and that in the chancy light of the lamp.

'Last October time, you say? Thinking on, I do recall something. It's this hair of hers, the colour of ripe corn. A carrier's cart went by with a young woman riding passenger. That was far from usual and I watched a moment. She turned to look at the mine.'

'Did she have a troubled air?'

'Sir, I couldn't say. The carrier whipped up the horse and they were gone.'

'One more thing.' Rudge returned the miniature to his pocket. 'Where does this road lead to?'

'Salter's Lane? It goes to Nantwich eventually, though there is a turning for Tarporley. That will be where the carrier was heading. Happen he dropped the young woman off at an inn. You might try the Swan. It's a posting house and well attended.'

'My thanks, sir. You've been a good help.'

★ ★ ★

Rudge lost no time in heading out there, keeping to tracks in the snow made by other travellers. It was slow journeying and the church clock was striking midday as he rode into the surprisingly empty inn yard. The bad weather was clearly having a detrimental effect on trade.

'Ho there. Anybody home?' Rudge hollered, dismounting.

The back door of the inn opened to reveal a tow-headed youth gorging on a large wedge of pie of some description. He came unwillingly across to Rudge.

'See to my horse, will you, lad. Give him a feed.'

'Oats is one shilling extra,' the lad said, spewing pastry crumbs as he spoke.

'So be it. Is the master about?'

'Aye. In the taproom.'

He jerked a thumb in that direction and took the horse, clopping off towards the stables.

After an excellent meal of veal pie and pickles, washed down by strong ale, Rudge again presented the miniature and asked his questions.

Bertram Cotterill gave a nod.

'Aye, that's Emmie all right.'

Rudge did not miss the shifty look in the man's eye.

'She worked here?'

'For a short while, aye.'

'Could you be more specific? Was she a reliable servant?'

'Us thought so. Then she upped and left.'

Rudge fixed the landlord with a steely gaze over the rim of his tankard.

'Did she give a reason?'

'No, and I dinna ask. What is this, any road? Has Emmie done summat?'

'Emma Trigg has gone missing. I'm investigating her disappearance on behalf of her family.' Rudge swigged down the last of his ale.

'One more thing, landlord,' he said mildly. 'Do you recall whether it was snowing when Emma left this establishment?'

'Well, I dunno. Happen it could have been flurrying a bit.'

'And she still went? Even though the weather looked bad?'

Bertram Cotterill shrugged.

' 'Twere up to her, wunnit? Now, sir, I must be off. There's no stage with the road south being snowbound, but I still have work to do.'

'I, too, shall be making tracks. My thanks, landlord.'

Rudge slapped down his payment for his own and his horse's repast on the bar, and left the inn.

A cold and foggy dusk had gathered by the time a knock sounded on the door of the house on Saddler's Row.

Maisie sprang to her feet in eager anticipation.

'That will be Master Rudge. I'll fetch him in.'

For once, the shop had closed early. Everyone was gathered in the front parlour. A fire had been lit and Rudge, bringing with him a waft of the bitter outdoors, went straight to the hearth to warm himself, spreading his chilled hands before the blaze.

A few moments were spent in greetings and making the introductions between Rudge and the two younger members of the family, after which Maisie set about seeing to their guest's comfort.

'Sir, you must be ready for some refreshment. Will you take some tea?'

'I'll not say no, mistress,' Rudge said gratefully.

Seated by the fire with a steaming cup of tea, a platter of beef sandwiches and another of seed cake on the low table between them all, Rudge launched into a review of the day.

'The landlord of the Swan wasn't giving anything away. Coming out, I bumped into a servant girl and had a word with her. I suspect she knew more than she was letting on. Likely she'd been primed to hold her tongue.'

Gideon Trigg cleared his throat noisily.

'You didn't believe what the landlord said?'

'No, sir, I did not. I've been in this line of work too long not to know evasion when I see it. To my mind, your granddaughter was dismissed for some reason. Likely she was turned out in that bad snowfall we had.'

Maisie clutched at her throat in dismay.

'Oh, no!'

'No one could have survived that,' Alfie muttered.

Hamilton gave a troubled murmur of agreement.

'No, indeed.'

'We don't know that for sure,' Gideon said staunchly. 'Hast any more news, Rudge?'

'None, sir, though I have thoughts on the matter. What of your granddaughter's relatives on her mama's side? The Dawnes of Mollington. Could she have gone to them for refuge?'

Maisie shook her head.

'It's unlikely. She was only a child when her mama passed on. Too young to know about her background and I . . . well, my father and I thought the least said the better.'

'So she doesn't know who they are. I see. Well, that eliminates that line of enquiry for now. What of her natural sire? He was a seaman. Was his ship a merchant vessel or military?'

'We cannot say for sure,' Maisie said. 'The story was that he was a midshipman working his ticket to the Americas, but that could just be hearsay. I can supply the name of the ship. It was the *Lady Grey*.'

Rudge was listening attentively.

'Would he have sailed from Plymouth?'

'Very likely,' Gideon Trigg said. 'Verity visited Plymouth quite a bit. Her people had relatives there. That'll be where she met him — the bounder!'

'We don't know for certain that he was, sir. Better to give a suspect the benefit of the doubt until proven otherwise,' Rudge said mildly.

He turned again to Maisie.

'Mistress Catchpole, you say your niece was made aware of her true papa only minutes before she left. She could have headed south in the vain hope of finding out about him.'

'That's a long shot,' Hamilton put in.

Again the quiet rebuke.

'Not necessarily. You'd be surprised how often the most slender clue can lead to a solution.' Rudge paused. 'A journey to

Plymouth would be time-consuming and costly. Master Trigg, do you wish me to pursue this case?'

Gideon threw an enquiring glance at the gathered company. It was nods all round.

'Aye, Rudge. Go ahead. Us'll never rest if us gives up now. How soon can you leave?'

'As soon as the roads become passable again,' Rudge said. 'This snow has caused havoc everywhere. The London Post isn't able to travel and the route onward to the coast will be even worse. They always get it bad in those parts.

'Rest assured, the moment my way is clear I shall head for Plymouth.'

Rudge picked up the monogrammed kerchief found in the feed loft at the Bickerton yard, which he had placed on the table.

'If you don't mind, I shall retain this for now. It may just come in useful.'

That settled, Maisie made fresh tea and offered the hitherto untouched food, which Rudge fell upon with relish.

After he had gone, Gideon's stoicism deserted him.

''Twill be a miracle if he finds her.'

Alfie went to his grandfather's side.

'Bear up, Granfer. I'm putting my faith in Sylvester Rudge.'

'I am of the same inclination,' Hamilton said.

Maisie made a gesture with her hand.

'Please God he's successful. I pray that Emma will soon be returned to us.'

'Amen to that,' Gideon endorsed heavily.

The usual words hung between them. Where was Emma?'

* * *

'Please . . . where is this?'

Emma's eyes fluttered open to meet the lively nut-brown gaze of a person several years older than her — a countrywoman, by her wind-burnished cheeks and air of staunch capability.

The woman tucked a straying frizz of brown hair back into her crumpled matron's cap and gave Emma a smile of encouragement.

'My stars, you's with us at last! Not before time, either. Emma — it is Emma, inna it? There's been so many names on your lips I'm all in a heap wi' them. This is Shepherd Coles's cottage at Peckforton. I'm Sarah Coles. My man came across you in the big snow we had. You'd come to grief in a fall and must have struck your head on a rock . . . no, dunna you touch it. Tes bound up but healing well.'

Beyond the small, deep-set window, children were engaged in noisy play.

'Mam, is her awake? Can us see?' pleaded a small figure from the doorway.

'Not now, our Annie. Go tell Da the glad news. Take the others with you. Give us some peace, there's a good lass.'

The excited babble faded gratifyingly into the distance. Emma moved her head, wincing as pain knifed through it, and took a tentative look around her.

She was in a cluttered house-place with much evidence of make-do-and-mend. Over a snapping wood fire a cauldron gave off an enticing smell of meat and herbs.

She tried to recollect what had happened.

'There was a blizzard — I couldn't see my hand in front of me. I remember reaching out. Then falling.'

'You tumbled, right enough. Clean over the edge of the quarry, you must have gone. My man were out there looking for a stray sheep with the dogs. 'Twere them found you. You took a fever — three days tes been. But there . . . ' A cool, dry hand felt her brow. 'Tes gone now.'

Emma closed her eyes again, trying to shut out the echo of the bad dreams that had come and gone in the throes of tormented sleep. What secrets had she unwittingly disclosed?

Her head pounded painfully, laying a veil over her brain, making it impossible to think. She moistened her dry lips.

'Here, have a sip o' water.'

A strong arm supported her while she drank. The well water was cool and refreshing. Emma shut her eyes and fell instantly into a deep, healing sleep.

When she awoke again darkness had fallen and the family, five children and their parents, were sat at supper around a scrubbed deal table.

Memories now came rushing back with terrible clarity. Banishment, rejection, false accusation, all the horrors of a world turned unfairly against her.

A slight movement of her arm brought the familiar tiny jingle of the charm bracelet that still, wonderfully, encircled her wrist. Josh. Her heart lurched at the memory.

Tears gathered, sliding helplessly from beneath closed lids.

'Her's cryin',' an incredulous voice piped up in the sure knowledge that grown-ups never wept.

'Hush, our Tommie,' the child's mother said.

Emma felt that same calming hand on her arm.

'There, now. Tes weakness that's taken a

hold. What you need is a dish of good mutton broth. Husband, tuck this bolster behind her back while I lift her. That's right. Annie, pour me some of that broth.'

With food inside her Emma felt a little better. She was clad in a high-necked nightgown, obviously belonging to the mistress of the house.

'My clothes?'

'Washed and aired ready for you, never you fear.'

'I must not overstay my welcome,' Emma said, with a troubled glance at her hosts and the group of wide-eyed children that gathered around her bed. 'I fear I may have been an encumbrance long enough.'

'You're going nowhere until my Sarah deems it right,' the shepherd replied with rough kindness. 'Get your strength back, lass. Then we'll see.'

★   ★   ★

A week passed before Emma was on her feet again. It was a time of crippling weakness and easy tears. Several more days slid by before she ventured outside, feeling the bite of the February easterlies as she had never felt it before.

She drew her shawl more tightly around

her and breathed in welcome gulps of fresh air. Snug though the cottage was, the presence of many bodies, plus a cade lamb being hand-reared on the hearth, not to mention the fug from continued cooking and the drying of laundry before the fire, made the atmosphere in the house-place less than pleasant. Mercifully, her carpet bag containing her belongings had survived the fall with her, and she was not short of a change of clothes.

Emma was aware of how they hung on her bones. She had lost weight during her time at the inn, but now she was positively skeletal. A glance at her reflection in the well at the front of the cottage revealed unrecognisably gaunt cheeks and dark-shadowed eyes.

Slowly, however, her resilient young body recovered. The wholesome food and long periods of rest brought a return to her strength. Emma was overwhelmingly grateful to the shepherd's wife, who treated her well and never asked awkward questions. Sometimes her glance would go to the charm bracelet on Emma's wrist and a look of bland curiosity would cross her face, but nothing was ever said and Emma was glad of it.

Hiding away suited her state of mind. Here in the remoteness of Peckforton, no one could find her. No one could make promises they would not keep.

She did what she could to help around the place, but the housewifely disciplines impressed upon her by her Aunt Maisie, and soundly reinforced during her sojourn at the hostelry — 'Any breakages and it gets docked from your pay!' — appeared to have deserted her. All her old carelessness and apparent inability to perform the simplest task without it ending in disaster seemed to have returned.

Sarah Coles, pushed to the limits of her endurance at the dropped pots and other clumsiness, shook her head in despair and laughingly sent Emma out to entertain the children, which she did admirably with stories and little rhymes and nursery songs learned at her mother's knee.

March came in on a brisk wind, bringing swelling buds, joyful birdsong and rich smells of wet loam from newly ploughed tracts of ground.

'It's time I made a move,' Emma said as they sat by the fire one night.

The children were in bed and the couple had grown closer. Emma was gripped by the uncomfortable feeling of being in the way.

'No hurry, lass.' The shepherd knocked the dottle from his clay pipe and set about filling it with fresh tobacco. 'Though since you mention it, Sarah did chance on a place that might suit.'

His eyes sought those of his wife. Sarah pursed her lips as if in doubt, and then shrugged.

'Tes a mile or so further on from here, on the outskirts of Peckforton. A housekeeper-companion wanted.' She broke off, frowning in thought. 'I's warning you, Emma, her inna the easiest of bodies. There's many a one given up and left.'

Emma's mind flew uneasily to the question of her doubtful housewifely skills.

'There'll be servants for the general work,' Sarah Coles continued, guessing Emma's worries perfectly. 'You'd be responsible for the overseeing of the household and keeping the mistress happy. You'd be good at that. Tes a Mistress Rosamund Platt of Hillside House.'

Emma thought hard. She could scarcely impinge on the couple's goodwill for ever, another body in the already overcrowded little dwelling, sleeping on a pallet on the house-place floor and eating their food.

Peckforton was suitably off the beaten track to keep her presence hidden, which was a point in favour. Really though, when all was said and done, what choice had she?

'I'll take it,' she heard herself say, and felt an immediate trickle of what could have been foreboding travel down her spine.

7

'Name?'

Rosamund Platt sat behind a desk of polished rosewood in the library and fixed Emma with a gimlet glare. She was a stately figure in whispering black silk, a cap of gossamer Honiton lace upon her crown of iron-grey hair, the same creamy lace frothing at her cuffs and throat.

'Emma Verity Trigg, madam,' Emma replied.

There was the briefest of pauses.

'What age are you, Trigg?'

'I shall be one-and-twenty come June, madam.'

'Hmm. You are very young for the position.'

'With respect, madam, I cannot help my years, but those granted to me have not been spent in idleness. I was brought up to manage a home with efficiency. I am acquainted with the keeping of household accounts, the rules of cooking and cleaning and the art of dealing with tradesmen.'

'Are you indeed?' Faint amusement crossed the autocratic face. 'And where, might I ask, were these commendable attributes acquired?'

'It was at my grandfather's house ... '
Emma broke off, took a steadying breath and
launched into the narrative she had prepared.
'I left home under trying circumstances and
took a position as housemaid at an inn. I was
moving on to better myself when I met with
an unfortunate accident and — '

A flap of the thin, be-ringed hand silenced
the flow.

'Yes yes, I was aware of all that. The
shepherd's wife made sure I was suitably
informed. You are a fluent reader, I take it? I
shall expect to have the newspaper read to me
each morning. My eyes, you know. I also have
a liking for the works of the Brontë sisters.
You are familiar with their writings?'

In fact Emma was not, but she felt she was
about to have the matter redressed when
handed a copy of *Agnes Grey* and instructed
to read a passage aloud, which she did in a
voice that was sufficiently expressive as to
bring a nod of approval from across the desk.

Rosamund Platt gave her a searching look,
which brought a stab of unease. Emma had
been under the impression that the position
was assured on the grounds that nobody else
would want it. All at once she was having
doubts.

The moment passed. She was sent a
semblance of a smile.

'Well then, Trigg, I think you will suit me well enough. You are prepared to begin immediately? Splendid!' The practicalities were then touched upon. 'We are not a large household. My cook, Mrs Bates, will provide you with a set of keys and your uniform. There are two maidservants, Faith and Lettie, and the outside man, Aston, who sees to the horses. You are able to handle a trap?'

'Oh, yes'm!' Emma replied eagerly. 'I'm equally at ease in the saddle.'

'Is that so?'

There was another small, loaded silence, after which Emma was directed to the kitchen quarters to acquaint herself with the staff.

'Thank you, madam.'

Just in time she remembered to drop a dutiful curtsey, before making her escape.

Outside the heavy wood-panelled door of the library, she found that her legs were shaking. But she had done it. She had got the position.

For better or worse she was now housekeeper-companion to the indomitable Mistress Rosamund Platt of Hillside House.

★　★　★

Right from the start, Emma loved the old house. Filled with family treasures, it had

192

been built a century earlier into the gentle curve of the hillside and was flanked by gardens, a stable yard and a rambling hard-and-soft-fruit orchard. Plump and plodding Martha Bates took to Emma immediately, as did housemaids Faith, rosy-faced and smiling, and Lettie, a local girl with a pronounced squint, who could be relied upon to amuse them all handsomely with gems of local gossip.

Even Aston, a limping and surly individual who had been here longer than anyone could remember, found a good word for Emma once he had the measure of her ability with his great passion, the horses.

All in all, life had taken a turn for the better. Emma found the management of Hillside House well within her capabilities, gained an almost ridiculous pleasure from the jangling bunch of household keys hanging on a chain from her waist, and was well satisfied with her uniform of dark blue twilled poplin, frilled white apron and white cap with lace trim, feeling it an improvement on the drab garb inflicted generally upon domestic staff. Her elderly mistress was not the easiest, but Emma could cope with that.

What did give rise to concern was the odd unexpected probe into her background. Whereabouts had she been raised? What of her family? Was there no one she wished to visit on her afternoon off?

Emma answered as best she could, ever conscious of that sharp, unfathomable gaze, weighing her up. In the main, however, Hillside House kept her fully occupied, and she was able to overcome her fears and put her energies into her work.

Rosamund Platt spent the greater part of the morning writing letters to distant acquaintances and associates. One afternoon Emma was handed some of these to post.

'The walk will do you good, Trigg. You may take your ease and not hurry back. I shall be going for my nap shortly and shall not need you until teatime.'

Emma put on her pelisse and bonnet and set off happily in the early spring sunshine. The posting box would take her past the shepherd's cottage. She stood a chance of seeing Sarah and the children.

She had reached the end of the drive when her gaze fell on the topmost envelope in her hand. The direction, written in the mistress's graciously flowing script, gave Emma pause. The name of the addressee meant nothing to her but the famous port, Plymouth, seemed somehow significant. Why it should be so was a mystery, and after a moment or two she smiled at her foolishness and continued on her way.

Late March was here before Rudge was able to make the journey south. With the continued snowbound state of the roads and other business demands on his part, a certain degree of delay was inevitable, though understandably frustrating for his Saddler's Row clients.

He put the time to good use and managed to discover, after some diligent probing into official records to which he had access, the whereabouts of the Plymouth branch of the Dawne family, with whom Emma Trigg's mother had stayed on visits south.

On arrival at Plymouth he booked a room at the Fisherman's Arms on the Barbican — a wide waterfront paved with ancient granite setts, home to Plymouth's fish traders and teeming with life. Behind the harbour lay a confusion of narrow, cobbled streets and dim alleyways, unwisely traversed after dark but safely negotiable during daylight hours.

Rested after a comfortable night and having breakfasted well, Rudge shrugged on his greatcoat of thick brown felt, collected his grey beaver hat and the worn leather satchel which held his business details, and set off along the unfamiliar route to locate the address his research had yielded.

Everywhere rang to the sound of the oily slap of water against wooden jetties, the distant boom of the sea and the high, insistent keening of seabirds overhead. There was a smell of tar and brine, reminiscent of Chester, which also boasted a harbour and an abundance of baffling thoroughfares. More than once Rudge had to enquire the way from a passer-by, and was duly directed onwards, his heavy tread becoming more shambling as the sun rose in the sky and his best black boots started to pinch.

He came upon it at last: a pleasant, well-kept house behind tall railings, set back with others on a quiet square. His summons was answered by an elderly female servant.

'Sir? Can I help you?'

'I trust so.' Rudge removed his hat and produced his most charming smile. 'Would Mr Caspar Widdecombe be at home, mistress? I have need to speak with him.'

'Well . . . '

Indecision sat on the woman's face and Rudge, handing over his business card, continued hastily. 'Tell him I am here with regard to the late Verity Dawne.'

The servant shuffled off and was back promptly. Rudge was shown into a prettily furnished parlour, small and over-warm from the leaping flames of the fire that blazed in the grate. Sitting on a day couch was a dimpled, silver-haired woman in a gown of dove-grey tarlatan, a gauzy shawl about her shoulders. She had a sweet face, from which lavender-blue eyes surveyed Rudge with caution and perhaps a hint of curiosity.

Her husband, a once-handsome man whose expression also indicated some apprehension, lost no time in asking Rudge what this was all about.

Rudge, taking a proffered seat opposite the couple, explained.

'I am investigating the disappearance of one Emma Trigg on behalf of her family. They are goodly Chester folk, saddlers of some repute and well respected in the town. Miss Emma's mama, I am led to believe, visited here during her girlhood.'

A look passed between the couple.

'Ah, Verity,' the woman said on a sigh.

Her husband reached out and pressed her hand with sympathy.

'I think,' he said slowly to Rudge, 'that this may take some time. Perhaps a little light refreshment would be in order. Sir, your legs are younger than mine. Would you have the goodness, please, to go and pull the bell?'

Over an excellent mid-morning repast of coffee and delicious little iced pastries that Rudge's sweet tooth could not resist, he listened to what his host had to say.

'Mary-Jane and I were not blessed with children. Verity was the daughter we never had. She would have been eleven or twelve when she first spent the summer with us and she came every year after that. Fascinated by the harbour and the ships, she was. Said it was more interesting than the quayside at her home town. And ride? She was a fearless and accomplished horsewoman.'

Rudge learned how the Widdecombes' ostler, a man called Baxter, was enlisted to chaperone Verity whenever she rode out. It was inevitable that a bond was forged between the two.

'She grew into a very lovely young woman,' the wife put in. 'High-spirited and laughing. Her energy was boundless. She made us feel young again.'

Rudge hesitated, and then broached the delicate subject of the liaison with the unknown seafarer.

'There was an admirer, a mariner of some description. There were unfortunate consequences.'

Caspar Widdecombe nodded.

'That is so. A hard time it was for us. Mary-Jane and I felt responsible for what happened. But I swear, sir, the assignations were kept very quiet. Neither of us had an inkling of what was going on.'

'Not an inkling,' Mary-Jane endorsed, with a nervous glance at her spouse.

Rudge again paused.

'I fear I must be frank here. If you would prefer to leave us, madam?'

'No, no.' The plump white hands fluttered in negation. 'Nothing can be done for Verity now, God rest her dear soul. But this — Emma, you say? This is her daughter.'

She looked beseechingly at her husband.

'Caspar, we must endeavour to assist Mr Rudge all we can.'

'Of course, my love.'

Caspar Widdecombe delivered her hand another tender gesture before resolutely meeting Rudge's gaze.

'Baxter would be your best chance. I always suspected the old rogue knew more about what went on than he was willing to say. Unfortunately, the years have caught up with him and he's no longer in our service. You will find him at the address I shall give you. 'Tis a fisher cottage on the seafront.'

Rudge delved into his satchel for the slim, leather-bound book in which he kept his notes. As he took down the details he experienced a familiar tingling of nerve endings that generally signified an encouraging move forwards.

Baxter was bent and wheezing, a shrivelled walnut of a fellow with a thin, bony face and the glint of humour in his rheumy old eyes. Rudge took him to a tavern on the waterfront, and with the ostler's tongue suitably loosened by strong ale he learned all he could about the young Verity Dawne.

'Like sunshine after rain, she were,' Baxter said in his slow, gentle West Country drawl that had probably soothed more horses than the man could count. 'Folk fell at her feet and I were no exception, I makes no excuses for thaat. Loved the 'orses, she did. Right from being a liddel maiden she'd come seeking me out in the stables. 'Saddle up, Baxter,' she'd say. 'Let's go for a gallop.' A proper job she made of it and all. She could make any 'orse move as if it had suddenly sprouted wings. Kind hands, she had — thaas the mark of a true horsewoman, and no mistake.'

He went on in this vein for some time.

'What of the young man?' Rudge asked at last, taking advantage of a pause while Baxter took several deep swigs of his drink.

'The sailor, you's meaning? Well now, I were wondering when thaat'd crop up. I gave Miss Verity my word not to say anything, but there, she be gone now — God rest her.

Besides, who's to say she'd not thank me if this helps her liddel maiden?

'They met at a midsummer ball and continued to see each other over the summer. I reckon they must have kept up a secret correspondence after Miss Verity went back home. Doan you ask me how she managed it. This were Miss Verity. She had a way of getting round folks.'

Baxter took a final gulp of his drink. Rudge indicated to the girl to furnish them with another flagon.

'So the pair kept in touch clandestinely over the winter months, and resumed their acquaintance when Verity came south again for that last summer?'

'Thaas about the sum of it. Mind you, he'd have been away at sea between times. He were back when she arrived that final June, though. Up with the lark she were, riding out of town to meet him, me following at a discreet distance.'

'Was she not aware of the danger of such a liaison?'

'Think you I didden warn her? She laughed. 'Don't be so stuffy, Baxter,' she'd say. Crazed wi' love for him, she were. Happy as the day is long.'

The flagon arrived. Rudge refilled the ostler's empty tankard.

'Did you ever meet him yourself?'

'Eh? No. I only had glimpses of him. He seemed a fine upstanding young fellow to me. The sort any man would be proud to see his daughter wed to.'

'He was an officer in the Royal Navy?'

'Wudden say thaat. 'Twere a cargo ship he sailed off in on that last voyage. The *Lady Grey*. Bound for the Americas with bales of cloth from up north and a load of other cargo, she were. 'Twere said she never arrived at port.'

'So I believe. How was Verity after he had sailed?'

'Proper downcast, she were. 'Twere the only time I ever saw her weep, as if she sensed she'd not see him again. Oh, doan' get me wrong. He were no bounder, nothing like thaat. Liddel things her let slip, well, like I's already said, he were a respectable sort. She wore his ring on a strip o' ribbon round her neck. Diamonds and rubies — a family piece, she said 'twaas.'

'Well connected, then. There was clearly talk of a union between them,' Rudge said thoughtfully.

'Must have been. A fine couple they'd have made, too.'

Silence fell, into which intruded the talk and laughter of the crowded taproom.

'I don't suppose you have the fellow's name?' Rudge asked.

'Ah, there you got me.' The wizened old face puckered in thought. 'I never was one for remembering names. Something like Guidman or Goodbone, it were. Any more liquor in the pot?'

Rudge reached for the flagon. The lead that had looked so promising was threatening to pall. Before he left for Chester, however, he would visit the harbour authorities and see if he could trace the ship from their records.

There were also other avenues to pursue. He had a mind to look up Emma's girlhood friend, Alice Courtney. According to Mistress Catchpole, an interview with the lass purported to be outside his jurisdiction, but there were always ways and means . . .

As the two men had been speaking, a silent figure in a dim corner, feasting alone on the house speciality of fish pie and crusty bread, watched them attentively. His meal finished, he rose and left the tavern.

★   ★   ★

Early morning sunshine lit the park. Alice passed through the entrance with her Pomeranian trotting beside her. She was about to take her usual route to the bandstand, when a figure stepped out from the shadows of the shrubby laurels by the path.

Alice started back in alarm, but fright turned quickly to joy when she saw who it was.

'Hamilton! How you startled me!'

He gave her a smile.

'My apologies. Alice, I hoped to find you here. May I walk with you a little way?'

'By all means.'

Alice wished she had worn her tawny day dress and mantle rather than the powder-blue, which she felt was somewhat draining to the complexion.

Beneath the tightly-laced confines of the deplored powder-blue bodice her heart thudded wildly. What did Hamilton want? Was he having second thoughts about her?

'I confess I've missed you,' he said as they fell into step, taking an uphill path that led between borders ablaze with spring flowers towards a seated balcony, approached by a flight of stone steps and overlooking the Dee and greening water meadows.

'And I you,' Alice said carefully. Some inner voice warned caution.

She waited for Hamilton's next words, and then could have wept with impatience when mere pleasantries escaped his lips.

They reached their destination and finding the area gratifyingly deserted, sat down and spent an awkward few moments contemplating the sun pennies on the rippling waters of the river below.

Hamilton then spoke.

'Alice, may I be blunt?'

'Of course. What is it?'

'I want to ask you if you have any notion at all of Emma's whereabouts. No, let me finish. I gathered from something Alfie inadvertently said that you may know more about Emma's involvement with Brookfield than any of us.'

'We talked, Emma and I. Of course we did.'

'When you brought Brookfield's letter to Granfer's attention, what were your motives? Not those of a loyal friend, I vow.'

Alice was silent. She hadn't expected this. She felt trapped between a rock and a hard place. Tell all, and she risked losing Hamilton totally.

On the other hand, he had admitted missing her. That surely counted for something. It seemed that if she stood any chance of winning Hamilton back she would have to be open with him.

She straightened her back.

'I confess I did Emma a wrong and I'm not proud of it. I told Master Trigg that Josh and

Emma were lovers. It wasn't true. Of course it wasn't. Yet he believed me. It surprised me how readily.'

Hamilton nodded, his face pained.

'In truth there were other factors involved. Granfer jumped to conclusions.'

Alice swallowed.

'I deliberately misled him. I could see how Emma was falling in love with Josh. I knew it before she did herself. Her face lit up when she spoke of him. I saw them together and I, well, I was envious.

'It wasn't like that with Alfie and me. There was no magic to speak of. I happened to say something to him about Emma that had him thinking. That was what put an end to the betrothal.'

'I gathered as much. Is that everything? Granfer sorely regrets his treatment of Emma. He's employed a private investigator to find her. She was traced to an inn at Tarporley. It is believed she left prior to the severe blizzard we had in January. Since then, nothing.'

Alice felt a huge tide of guilt well up inside her. Her face crumpled. She held the warm little figure of the dog closely to her for comfort and between great gulps of breath, told Hamilton about her encounter with Josh Brookfield and what had transpired since.

'Hamilton, I knew you'd be searching for Emma. I thought if Josh could find her first he'd seek you out privately and put in a good word for me, and that would make everything right between us again.'

She dragged in another quivering breath.

'I didn't mean it all to go so disastrously wrong. And now Emma might be dead and it's my fault and I don't blame you if you never want to see me again!'

It was too much. Alice turned away and wept as she had never wept before.

Then, unbelievingly, she felt Hamilton's arms steal reassuringly around her.

'Hush,' he said softly. 'We are all to blame in part for Emma's disappearance; none more so than Granfer. But, Alice, he's doing all he can to rectify it. This investigator, Rudge, is currently following a line of enquiry in Plymouth. We must put our faith in him.'

She raised a blotched, tear-stained face to his.

'You forgive me in spite of everything?'

He pressed a kiss on her forehead, on each cheek, on the tip of her nose.

'Alice, I love you,' was his response.

It seemed to say all. He drew her head on to his shoulder.

For a while they just sat there on the park bench, content to be together, while on the river below a herd of mute swans made its stately procession downstream, leaving a tide of ever-increasing ripples in its wake.

★　★　★

It was market day at Chester, a morning of fickle April sunshine and showers. Josh rode along Brook Street with a string of horses to trade. Tomorrow, he would speak with Alice. With any luck there could be word of Emma.

Many times he had returned, ever eager for news, only to have his hopes cuttingly dashed. His trading had taken him to the most lucrative sales in the country; the small, padlocked and iron-bound coffer that held his gold was full. He had more than enough to fund his goal and buy a property and land suited to his purpose. What he needed was Emma at his side to help choose it.

He rode into the throbbing heart of the venue, thinking of Emma as he tethered the horses. Her chaotic charm and merry smile, the sweet colour that came and went in her cheeks, the bright brown eyes and tumble of corn-gold hair, her irrepressible eagerness for life . . . Emma. She had to be here, somewhere.

Trading that day was swift and the hours marched on.

At noon, with five of his string sold and one yet to go, he broke off to purchase a pasty and a cup of ale from a street vendor close to the auctioneer's rostrum.

He had finished the meal and was throwing a glance around for the ragged urchin who earned a penny collecting in the used tin cups and plates for the vendor, when a figure in tawny caught his attention.

Alice Courtney.

She saw him at once and hurried over, her fashionably wide, hooped skirts swishing as she came.

'Josh. I've been looking all over for you.'

'Good day, Alice.' Hope leapt in his heart. 'You've news?'

'Of sorts, yes. Oh, nothing of Emma. At least, not yet.'

Josh listened, his eyes never leaving her face, while she explained how she had encountered Hamilton and made her confession to him.

'I'm not proud of what I did,' she said in a tone that for Alice was decidedly humble. 'I'm sorry if I misled you into thinking I was acting entirely within Emma's interest. The truth is, Emma and I had had a falling out. It was because of the way I was treating Alfie at the time. Emma took me to task over it and, oh, it's all very involved and silly. Suffice to say I've acted abominably.'

Her voice faltered; she lowered her eyes. She went on to tell Josh about the Triggs' move to enlist the services of a private investigator.

'The man is at Plymouth at the moment, but when he returns Hamilton has elected to speak with him on my behalf. Well, he's only thinking of me. So disconcerting for a girl, to be caught up in this. Dear Hamilton has my best interests at heart.'

Alice's confession came as no surprise to Josh. She went on to say how supportive Hamilton was being towards her, how kind and understanding, but here Josh cut her short. His concern was Emma.

'Plymouth? Why so?'

'The investigator — Rudge, Hamilton calls him — sniffed out a clue to her whereabouts there. Josh, Hamilton sends a message. If you should come across any information on Emma, would you please get in touch with them?'

Josh made a sharp gesture of impatience with his hand.

'I did. I was turned away, though I dare say there's been a change of attitude since.'

'Indeed,' Alice said gravely. 'Master Rudge seems very skilled in his line of work. He'd followed Emma's trail to the Swan, though he did not get as much information out of the innkeeper as you.'

'That's understandable. Two people turning up asking questions? The man would have been on his guard. Did this Rudge find anything else? Had he checked for human remains after the snow had gone?'

'He did so. I overheard the matter being discussed at one of Mama's afternoon-tea gatherings. One cannot keep a matter like this secret and people love to gossip. But never mind that.' Alice's eyes gleamed. 'There was nothing. Josh, it means she's still alive.'

'I never doubted it for one moment,' Josh said.

'I know you didn't.' She took a step back. 'Well, that is all I have to say. Let us hope things are soon resolved.'

He watched her walk away and thought what a troublemaking little miss she was. How callous was the hand of fate, when the innocent were at the mercy of persons more fortunate than themselves.

'Ho there, Brookfield. Good day to you.'

Josh came out of his reverie to find a long-term customer at his side, a farmer of middle years with lands to the north of the Whitchurch turnpike.

'Good day, sir. Are you well?'

'Aye, fair to middlin'. I'm seeking a riding

nag,' the farmer said. 'Hast anything that will suit?'

'Is it a cob you are after? I've one here. A handsome 15 hands high liver chestnut. Eight years old, sound in wind and limb, steady as a rock. Want to try him out?'

The deal made with every success, Josh dropped the farmer an enquiry with regard to the snowbound winter and lost persons.

'Now you mention it, there was talk at the Three Foxes at the time. 'Twere a shepherd came across someone in a snowdrift. Still breathing, 'twas said. Well, just about.'

Josh's heart leaped.

'Can you tell me more? Was the victim male or female?'

The man shook his head.

'Nay, lad, I canna say. 'Twere nobbut passing gossip, you understand. Whoever it were sounded in a bad way to me. Chance is the poor wretch is dead and buried by now.'

Josh inwardly cursed with frustration. If this was Emma she could still be in the area. In which case it would do no harm to ride out there yet again and see if he could put meat on the bones of what he hoped was not purely tavern talk.

★ ★ ★

The spring day was dwindling to dusk by the time Josh had ridden the full extent of the turnpike, halting now and again to make enquiries with travellers on the road.

All to no avail.

At length Josh turned Black Diamond for his Flookersbrook lodgings. Luncheon was a distant memory and hunger gnawed at him. He trusted Mistress Bradely had something good cooking. With food inside him he would be more able to get his thoughts in order.

Dark had fallen before he reached the stable yard. Dismounting, Josh glanced up at the sky and thought how faint the stars were against the glow of city lamps.

One, however, gleamed brighter than the rest. He wondered if Emma was seeing that same twinkling star. He sent a worshipful wish that he would find her before long.

* * *

Emma breathed in the fragrance of early apple blossom in the sheltered orchard of Hillside House and looked up at the stars. How bright they were. How they glimmered in the deep velvet of the sky.

One was particularly noticeable. Unbidden, her thoughts went to Josh. She had elected to banish him from her mind and in the main, by filling her days with work and falling exhausted into bed at night, had succeeded. Tonight, however, his face was so clear that he might almost be standing here at her side.

She recalled the intense blue of his eyes, the roguish twinkle, the smile that had seemed for her alone, and she sighed and her heart twisted in pain.

Contrarily perhaps, she still wore the charm bracelet. It had become so much a part of her she could not discard it — or so she told herself.

Yesterday, accompanying her mistress to matins at Holy Trinity Church in Bickerton, she had worn her mother's cameo brooch at the throat of her blouse.

The mistress had asked her about it.

'It was my mama's, madam,' she answered.

The pony, a lively little beast, chose that moment to test her out and started to jib and jink, putting an end to conversation. The trap bounced alarmingly, jostling the passengers. Her mistress let out a cry of distress and all Emma's attention was taken up with bringing the animal back under control.

On reaching the small country church in the hills, she fastened the pony to one of the iron tethering rings on the sandstone wall and helped her mistress to disembark. Before following her up the churchyard path, she paused at a grave close to the gate.

Her old friend Sam Brookfield lay there, together with the young wife he had so cherished.

It had been a shock that first time. Now, Emma had come to terms with it. What continued to upset her was the bareness of the plot compared to others and she had taken to leaving a small posy of wayside flowers there. This time it was white violets, still in bud and sweet with the drenching scents of springtime.

Emma turned her thoughts to this morning, when something untoward had happened.

The house was a rabbit warren of ill-lit passages. She had taken one of these, with an armful of laundry on the way to the linen cupboard, when on the wall a small painting in an elaborate oval frame that had hitherto escaped her notice pulled her up short.

It was a portrait of a young woman. She had lively brown eyes and her lips were curved into a faint smile that hinted at mischief. Apart from the elaborately styled and powdered hair and low-squared bodice suggestive of an earlier age, Emma might have been looking at an image of herself.

Baffled and shaken, she was not aware of the figure coming along the passage until the tap-tap-tap of her mistress's ebony cane brought her to her senses.

Rosamund Platt came to a stop beside her.

'So, Trigg, you have found her. I wondered how long it would be.'

'Madam, I don't understand.' Emma darted another bemused glance at the portrait. 'Please, could you tell me who she is?'

'Willingly. Though not at this moment, I vow. You have your duties to perform, besides which 'tis too involved a matter to discuss here. Come to me this evening. I will explain all I can.'

The cultured tones were kindly. Emma was given a small smile, after which her mistress continued along the passageway, leaving Emma standing there with the bundle of freshly laundered bed linen still clutched in her arms.

On and off throughout the day she had pondered on what might be in store. Now, the first throaty warble of a nightingale reminded that evening was here and the mistress would be expecting her.

Her heart in her mouth, she left the orchard that was now pearled with dew, and went to hear what Rosamund Platt had to say.

★ ★ ★

'That is all I learned from the Widdecombes' groom,' Rudge said to the gathered company in the parlour of the house on Saddler's Row. 'It does paint a more favourable picture of the young man who was Emma's sire, methinks.'

'Yes, it does,' Maisie agreed.

''Tis beside the point,' Gideon said brusquely. 'By all account the fellow's long been food for the fishes. Didst consult the harbour master, Rudge?'

'I did, sir, and traced the ship in question. As the groom said, the *Lady Grey* was a cargo vessel bound for the Americas with cloth from Yorkshire and other sundry items besides. The ship was believed wrecked at sea with all hands.'

'Ah me!' Maisie shook her head sorrowfully. 'God rest their souls.'

'I took the opportunity of making a note of the names of the crew.' Rudge drew a folded sheet of paper from his leather satchel, handing it to Gideon. 'As you will see, sir, there is no Guidman or Goodbone, as suggested by Baxter. But then, he did say his memory was not the best for names and this was many years ago. Goodly is the closest, of which there are three. One was a boy so can be ruled out. There was also Jerome, ship's carpenter, and a Nathaniel Goodly, officer. Both were in their mid-twenties, so either could have been our man.'

Alfie gave a snort of impatience.

'This is leading nowhere. How can a person long dead be of any assistance?'

'I could try and trace the man's family,' Rudge replied mildly. 'There is the possibility of your sister having discovered who her true sire was and gone on to contact his people.'

'A slim chance,' said Hamilton, frowning in doubt.

'But a chance all the same. Believe me, stranger things have happened. I shall also make it my concern to contact Emma's maternal relatives, if possible. That is, with your permission, sir.'

Gideon gave Rudge a nod.

'Whatever you think. Us can't stop now . . . though I have to agree with the boys. This has become something of a conundrum.'

The long-cased clock in the hallway struck the hour.

Rudge looked up.

'Seven of the clock. I must be keeping you good people from your evening meal. I shall continue with my enquiries and be in touch. Say, a week from now?'

'As you will,' Gideon said.

'Then I'll bid you all goodnight.' Rudge

stood up and Maisie made to rise and see him out, but was intercepted by Hamilton. 'Be easy, Mama. I'll attend to Master Rudge.'

The two men left the room. There was a murmured conversation in the hallway, followed by the shutting of the front door, then Hamilton's voice.

'Is that pot roast I can smell? I can't speak for anyone else, but I'm ready for some supper.'

*   *   *

They were halfway through the meal when there was a loud rapping on the front door.

Maisie put down her knife and fork.

'Who can that be? Not Rudge, surely? Perhaps he forgot to tell us something.'

'I'll go and see,' Hamilton said.

On the step was a tall figure, his face in shadow in the darkness of the Row.

'Good evening, sir,' the stranger said in a voice that held a trace of West Country speech. 'My apologies for disturbing you, but would this be the residence of Gideon Trigg the Saddler?'

'It is, sir,' Hamilton said. 'Though I fear the shop is closed until the morrow.'

'That isn't what I've come about. I have reason to believe that the daughter of Verity

Dawne has connections here. My interest is somewhat more than a passing one. My name is Nathaniel Goodly. Captain Nathaniel Goodly, at your service.'

8

After a moment of stunned surprise, everyone rallied. Maisie, inwardly thankful that the pot roast would go round, invited the unforeseen guest to join them for supper. Alfie brought up a chair to the table. While they supped the talk was kept to pleasantries, though the tension in the air was almost palpable.

Meal over, Hamilton built up the fire in the parlour and the company settled around it. Eyes turned expectantly upon the man who had presented himself as Captain Nathaniel Goodly. The name had touched a chord with them all. It was on Rudge's list of crew members aboard the doomed *Lady Grey*.

'Firstly,' Captain Goodly said, arranging his long legs before the blaze and steepling his strong, sun-browned fingers. 'I must make it clear that I loved Verity deeply and I believe my feelings were returned. I make no excuses. We were young and foolish and I took that love for granted. But I was no hapless Jack Tar. I had every intention of formally requesting Verity's hand in marriage on my return from the voyage to America. I would add that I come from reputable seagoing stock. My father captained his own ship and from a boy I wanted the same. It was a training ship for me and then off to sea as a deck officer. I had just gained that status when I met Verity.'

'That should have been acceptable enough for the Dawnes,' Gideon put in dryly.

'Verity believed so. She wore my ring.'

Maisie gave a nod.

'I have a box containing Verity's personal effects. Doubtless the ring is there. Her cameo brooch went to Emma on her twelfth birthday. It felt fitting that she should have some memento of her mama. The rest she was to have on her marriage.'

It struck Maisie how like Emma their guest was, translated into more masculine lines. Same intelligent brown eyes, same thick mane of fair hair, bleached here almost to white by relentless foreign suns. Captain Goodly sported a seafarer's beard and was dressed, not in naval uniform as one might have expected, but a well-cut travelling suit of dark-blue worsted, the plainest of linen with starched cravat, and black leather boots well polished.

Maisie indicated for him to continue.

'In brief, we met with rough seas off the coast of Newfoundland. The ship was over-laden with cargo. She stood not a chance and went down with all hands, bar a lad and myself. We somehow made it to the shore. A fisherman found us, both more dead than alive from cold and exhaustion. His wife, good woman that she was, nursed us back to health. As soon as he was able the lad joined a passing wagon train heading inland. I stayed on and helped with the fishing. I felt I owed them that.'

Captain Goodly made a spreading gesture with his hands.

'Likely you can see how it was. No money, personal papers, nothing. All my possessions had gone down with the ship and this place was remote, with precious little contact with the outer world. I wrote Verity a letter and gave it to a traveller to put on a ship bound for home. It's doubtful she ever received it.'

'It was assumed everyone aboard the *Lady Grey* was lost,' Gideon said.

A look of pain crossed the captain's handsome face.

'How despairing Verity would have been at that.'

He had eventually worked his passage home, by which time he learned that Verity was wed and the mother of an infant girl.

'I always wondered at the parentage of that child.'

'I think, if you were to see Emma, that

would solve any doubts,' Gideon said.

'By heaven, what I'd give to meet her! I named my ship the *Verity*. Happen the next should be the *Emma*.'

'You are ambitious, sir,' Gideon said.

'Aye, well, I never married. Verity was my only love. When I chanced to overhear that conversation between your man and the fellow I recognized as the Widdecombes' groom, well, I felt compelled to follow things up.'

'Praise be you did,' said Alfie, who had remained wide-eyed and silent until now.

Hamilton likewise agreed.

Gideon's eyes met Maisie's in question. She gave him a nod. Gideon reached for his pipe and tobacco.

'I reckon your credibility is assured, Captain Goodly. There remains the need for you to be acquainted with the details. 'Tis not all favourable, I fear. Wilt take a glass with us?'

'I will, sir.'

Maisie rose to attend to the task. Her mind was spinning. How extraordinary was the hand of fate. There was now more cause than ever to find Emma.

* * *

'Come in, child,' Rosamund Platt said to Emma. 'Sit here by me.'

Wonderingly, and not a little perplexed, Emma obeyed. This was the mistress's personal domain, a gracious, south-facing parlour comfortably furnished with easy chairs and low tables and smelling of lavender polish and the bowl of glass-house lilies that Emma had arranged that morning.

'I shall come straight to the point. I have reason to believe that you and I are related, albeit distantly. When first I set eyes on you I was struck by a resemblance to a young woman I knew as Verity Dawne. Your mama, it appears. Were you aware of a kinship with the Dawnes of Mollington?'

'No, madam.' Emma heard the surprise in her own voice. 'I knew my mama was well-connected, and that is all.'

'Hmm. What else have you been told?'

'Only a little. It all came out in rather a rush after I was in trouble with Granfer Trigg. Apparently the person I called Papa was not actually so.'

'That is quite correct. Verity spent her summers with relatives at Plymouth. It was here she met the man who was your father. I still correspond with the Plymouth people, the Widdecombes.'

Emma stiffened. She recalled the letter

directed to the seaport, the uncanny stirring in the blood it had evoked. Whether it was the place or the name she had no idea, but there had been a fleeting recognition. Was this, then, the reason?

'You are bewildered, child. As well you might be. Let us keep the explanations as simple as possible for now.' Rosamund Platt took a breath. 'Other issues made me realize there was more to this than pure coincidence. The name you shared with your mama — Verity. 'Tis a family name and the cameo brooch you wear is a family piece. What sealed the matter was the portrait you were studying earlier today. Your likeness to that young woman is remarkable. She was a great-aunt of your mama's, a beauty in her day.'

Rosamund Platt went on to say how she, like everyone else, had fallen under Verity's spell.

'She had such zest for life. She was ebullient and beautiful.'

'Yes, I remember. It cannot truly be said that I feature her. I'm no beauty. And I can be awkward in my ways. Bumbling, my Aunt Maisie called me.'

'Fie! As a girl your mama could never step into a room without sending something flying. I put it down to high spirits. As to the other — you do have a certain look of her.' Rosamund Platt paused, her eyes narrowing. 'I do not wish to pry, but I take it the 'trouble' with your grandfather involved a young man.'

'Yes,' Emma said painfully. 'We wanted to wed — at least, so I believed. It was never discussed but the feeling was there for both of us and things happened to thwart us. He — his name was Josh, Josh Brookfield — put an end to the association for my sake. There was a later chance encounter in which we both made our feelings clear. I'm sure Josh was going to approach the subject of marriage at a further meeting the following day only . . . Oh, it's all very involved. Suffice to say that Granfer Trigg came by some information and incorrect conclusions were drawn.'

'I see. Well then, let us hope for better things to come. You have grandparents at Mollington who live to regret their harsh treatment of their daughter. 'Twould be gratifying to see the family rift healed in the not too distant future.' Rosamund Platt again broke off, and then said tentatively, 'Was your mama happy, Emma?'

'I believe so. We lived above Papa's saddler's shop at Parkgate. Mama would take my brother and me for walks along the front and show us the boats. Then she and Papa took ill and died and Alfie and I went to live with Granfer Trigg and Aunt Maisie at Chester.'

Silence. The pretty ormolu clock on the mantelpiece ticked busily; a log collapsed in the grate in a shower of sparks.

Rosamund Platt straightened in her chair.

'So what now? One can hardly continue to address you as a servant. It shall be Emma in future — that is quite acceptable for a lady's companion, should it come under question. As to yourself, do you wish it to be known that you are a relative and call me Cousin Rosamund? The choice is yours.'

'I think, madam,' Emma said in a voice that shook, 'it might be best to leave matters as they are for now.'

Her fingers stole to the charm bracelet on her wrist and her heart panged. Her life had indeed taken an extraordinary upward turn. Nothing, however, could make up for the aching sense of loss she felt. Deep down, she knew that all she had ever really wanted was the man with the blue Irish eyes and a way with words like no other.

* * *

Josh entered the saddler's shop prepared for argument. Whatever it took, he had to see if any progress had been made over Emma. He was surprised and a little disconcerted to find that the man behind the counter was not Gideon Trigg as expected, but a much younger person.

Josh nodded a greeting.

'Good morrow. My name is Josh Brookfield.'

There was the briefest hesitation, and then the young man's personable face broke into a smile.

'Glad to meet you, sir. Alfie Trigg, Emma's brother.'

The two men shook hands across the counter.

'My grandfather and cousin are out on business. Can I be of help?' Alfie said.

'Possibly. I should say that I was not exactly welcome here when I last came.'

'I'm sorry about that. I think you will find that much has changed since then. This is about Emma, isn't it?'

'Aye. I must find her. She was last seen in the Tarporley district. I have searched unfailingly, combed every lane and byway but ah! the area is vast. It begins to feel an impossible task. If there is anything you can tell me, I would be grateful.'

'In fact there has been a new development. What do you know of Emma's background?'

'Her background? I don't care a whit for that! It's Emma I care about,' Josh said testily, and then had the uneasy sensation that he was not going to like what was coming.

'Were you aware that my grandfather engaged professional help to find my sister?'

'A man called Rudge, yes. Alice Courtney told me.'

'Alice did?' Alfie was taken aback.

'She and I have been in contact for some while. From what I could deduce, Alice had reasons of her own for wanting to sort out this dilemma.'

'That comes as no surprise,' Alfie said wryly. 'With regard to Emma's history . . . '

Josh listened, not interrupting, to what Alfie had to say. He heard about the uncertain paternity, the findings at Plymouth and their startling consequences. Lastly, he learned of Emma's maternal lineage and felt his heart clench perilously.

The question of Emma's sire bothered him not one jot. A seagoing career was a worthy enough calling and the fact that the fellow had come forward after all this time did him credit.

The connection on the mother's side was something else. She was too good for the likes of him, a trader with nothing to his name but a string of nags and a head full of dreams.

'The Dawnes,' he said, his voice choked and raw. 'I should have realized. That air about her, that easy confidence.'

'Emma has our mother's spirit,' Alfie put in. 'There's much of her sire in her, too.'

'You still have no idea of her whereabouts?'

'I fear not. We don't even know if she survived the hardships that befell her . . . ' Alfie's words trailed. He looked despondent.

'Emma lives. I know it!' Josh said fiercely.

'Your faith is encouraging. Perhaps we should join forces in this. Will you come through to the house, sir, and meet my aunt?'

Such a move was pointless. Josh gave his head a shake.

'My thanks, but I think not, all things considered. I had best go.'

He needed air. He had to think. He turned and blundered blindly for the door, leaving Alfie staring after him in utter bewilderment.

★   ★   ★

Within the hour Josh had packed his saddlebags, settled his bill at Flookersbrook and left, a recent acquisition of six horses trotting out in a string behind him.

There had been showers that morning and Black Diamond's iron-shod hooves rang out sharply on the wet surface of the road,

231

echoed by the pattering rush of the unshod string. A smell of fresh loam wafted from leys of newly ploughed ground on either side of the highway. Overhead, a skylark soared, singing, towards the mid-afternoon sun that was now shining fitfully over the fast-greening landscape.

As a rule, Josh welcomed the coming of spring. Today he was oblivious to the scents and sounds around him. His one thought was to pay his final respects to his loved ones and make his escape.

He urged his horse on and the string paced out accordingly, the drumming of hooves a relentless background to the painful pounding in his head. He came at last to the small country church in the fold of the hills. Josh flung his horse's reins over the standing post, tethered the string to one of the iron rings in the wall and entered the churchyard through the lychgate, his booted feet crunching on the pebbled path.

At the graveside, he froze. For there, by the headstone, was a posy of white violets.

White violets. One hand only could have put them there. In that moment his heart soared, as ecstatic as the skylark above him. Emma was alive! She was here after all, in this very vicinity. How, in heaven's name, during his countless forays of puddled lane and muddy byway, could he have missed her?

Not that it was any longer an issue, and despair broke over him afresh.

At his feet, the two who had given him life slept on in the final, eternal sleep.

'Why?' he raged aloud. 'Why should fate deal such a cruel blow?'

His father's answer rang in his head.

Dunna you take on so, lad. Stop dotherin' about and get you along after her. Talk with the lass, find out where her heart lies.

Would it were that simple.

Josh lingered there, lost in aching thoughts of what might have been, while beyond the church wall the horses cropped the wayside grass and the sun dipped lower in the west. High above, the skylark trilled on and Josh, catching the sound, had to wonder how anything could be so joyful when all felt so hopelessly black.

★ ★ ★

Rudge sat back in his chair, thoughtfully twirling the trimmed quill between his fingers. Before him on the desk was the Trigg ledger. He had been sifting through it in hope of finding some clue previously overlooked. So far, nothing.

Thanks to a gorgon of a housekeeper, his

endeavour to speak with the Dawnes had failed miserably. Alice Courtney had been less of a problem. She walked often in the park and had seemed all too ready to talk.

Rudge gave his lips a quirk. What a cartload of trouble that one had stirred, with her scheming and petty jealousies. It was extraordinary that Hamilton Catchpole had accepted her misdoings. Not many would have been so forgiving. He'd lay a pound to a penny that Gideon Trigg would not be, once he was acquainted with the full story.

Sunlight, slanting in through the high window, fell across the desk. Absently Rudge watched the dust motes dancing in its beam, whilst mentally picturing Emma's final moments with her family. He saw her distress, felt the hurt and shock at the revelation of her begetting. Maisie Catchpole had been obliged to speak in haste. What effect had the rushed words had upon the young woman?

His reverie was broken by the hail of the post boy outside the door. Rudge went to answer the summons and was handed three letters. The first two, bills, were tossed aside to be dealt with again.

The third bore a Plymouth postmark.

Rudge ripped the envelope open and

Caspar Widdecombe's name blazed up at him.

Tuesday 25th April, 1851

My dear sir,
  I am writing to inform you of something that may be pertinent to the matter close to the hearts of my dear wife and myself, and in which you have a professional interest. I recently received some correspondence from a relative at Peckforton, Cheshire. My cousin states that she took on a young lady companion who bore an uncanny resemblance to poor dead Verity. The young woman's surname (which would have meant nothing to my cousin) was Trigg.
  Sir, this may be of import to you. Should you opt to pursue the matter I am pleased to supply my relative's name and direction.

She is:
Miss Rosamund Platt
Hillside House
Peckforton
Cheshire

I remain your humble servant,
Caspar Widdecombe

The page shook slightly in Rudge's hand. Peckforton! The region was a veritable maze of tree-lined lanes that dipped and twisted and forked unexpectedly off into sandy tracks winding up into rugged, gorse-clad hills. Small wonder the young miss had remained so elusive, if indeed this was whom they sought.

Rudge left the letter among the clutter on the desk and went to stand by the window, gazing thoughtfully out at the busy street. Was he on the verge of running his quarry to ground at last?

Trigg was a common enough name hereabouts and lady's maids ten-a-penny. There had been so many false trails, such dashed hopes and disappointment. Was this to be yet another?

Faintly, at the back of his neck, Rudge felt that skin-prickling sensation that generally indicated a positive outcome. So be it. Other issues required his immediate attention. First thing tomorrow, he had a mind to saddle up for the mazy byways of Peckforton.

★ ★ ★

Alice tripped lightly along the Rows, heading for Rudge's place of work. For once, poor darling Suzette had been left behind. Dogs,

Master Rudge had confided, made him sneeze. Such a triviality would not normally have been a consideration but with events currently moving in her favour, Alice was prepared to make allowances.

A smile touched her lips. How she loved Hamilton. How wonderful to know that her love was returned. Alfie, too, was walking out with someone else — a huge relief.

The only cloud on her sunny horizon was Emma, hence the visit to the dingy little office on the Watergate.

On reaching the building, she tripped lightly down the corridor, rapped on the office door and went in, trying not to wrinkle her nose at the smell of dust, ink and stale tobacco smoke that assailed her.

Rudge was seated behind his desk, frowning over some papers. He rose at once with a polite word of greeting and made a move to get her a chair, which Alice declined prettily.

'No, no, please don't bother. I see you are far too busy to speak with little me.'

Rudge gave her his smile that never failed to impress.

'It is my pleasure. There we are. Pray be seated. What can I do for you, Miss Alice?'

'I've come about Emma,' she said, seating herself at the desk and loosening her bonnet strings in readiness to talk. 'I wondered if you had any news.'

'I have, in fact. Naturally, I can reveal nothing more until I have spoken to my clients.'

The curiosity that swept through Alice was all-consuming. She had to know what this was all about. She fluttered her eyelashes beguilingly.

'Please?'

'Nay, my dear, I have my loyalties to consider and — '

Some commotion out in the street caused Rudge to break off. He strode to the window, peering out.

Alice was quick. On the desk with other papers, she had already spotted the letter the man had been scrutinising. By craning her neck, she was able to read enough to capture the gist of it. There was an address which she made sure to commit to memory.

'Some fellow nearly met his end under the hooves of the brewery team,' Rudge said from the window. 'The traffic in this town gets worse.'

He turned to find Alice retying her bonnet strings for the off.

'I mustn't impose on your time a moment longer, sir,' she said sweetly, and left the office on a cloud of rose-scented air that played havoc with the investigator's sinuses and provoked a loud fit of sneezes that followed Alice all the way down the corridor to the exit.

The cathedral clock was striking four as she emerged from the building. She set off smartly for home. If this did happen to be Emma at the Peckforton house, the first to know should be Josh Brookfield. She'd best make haste, before Rudge beat her to it.

At home, she called out to her mama that she was taking the carriage and went to harness the horse. Alice's little dog was disinclined to be left behind a second time and escaped through the open door. She then got underfoot, yelping indignantly up at Alice as her mistress backed the horse into the shafts with the obvious intention of forsaking her.

'Suzette! You can't come, my poppet. You'll only be in the way . . . Oh, very well. In you get, but be warned. This will not be the most accommodating ride.'

Presently Alice was driving out into the clogged thoroughfare, fuming at the clot of tradesman's carts, drays and private vehicles in front of her. At the first opportunity she turned the horse into Dog Lane, a narrow route of overhanging buildings and blessedly free of traffic, and thence onto St John Street and a series of back roads which brought them, eventually, to the edge of town.

She then shook the reins for Flookersbrook, the carriage rattling and swaying as they pounded along the rutted road, the little dog joggling uncomfortably on the plush-lined seat beside her.

On reaching the lodging house, Alice disembarked hastily and, leaving her affronted pet in the carriage, sped to the main door of the house.

'I want to see Master Brookfield,' she said to the woman who answered her summons. 'It's imperative that I speak with him.'

The woman gave her head a shake.

'Nay, miss. You've just missed Master Brookfield. Him's paid up and gone — for good, him said.'

'Oh!' Alice could have wept in frustration. 'Which road did he take?'

'Headed for the hills, him did. Likely to pay his da's grave a last visit. Well, him wunna go without saying goodbye, not Master Brookfield. 'Tis Holy Trinity at Bickerton . . .'

Alice was already mounting the carriage, gathering up the reins. She galloped for the hills, her anxious gaze on the setting sun. Would Josh still be there?

Her relief to see the solid bulk of Black

Diamond and company of tethered horses outside the church wall was immense. Standing immobile by a grave close to the lychgate was Josh. His head was bowed, his shoulders slumped. Despair showed in every line of his person.

The little dog was not going to be left alone again in the hated vehicle. She leaped out with her mistress and went pattering on ahead in search of some sympathy at the unjust treatment she had received. Seeing the stranger, she went bobbing round his feet and barking shrilly up at him.

Josh, brought abruptly to his senses, met Alice's harassed gaze with obvious surprise.

'Alice! What brings you here? Here, pup. Go to your mistress.'

He scooped the dog up and Alice, snatching her pet in exasperation from him, tucked her unceremoniously under her arm.

'Josh. I must speak with you. You're surely not leaving?'

'I am.' He threw a glance at the fast-setting sun, at the lengthening shadow that crept across the churchyard, and shook his head in disbelief. 'I've been here too long. I should have been on my way long ago.'

'Where are you going?' Alice asked him.

'North. There's nothing for me here, not now.'

'Josh, there is everything. Emma has been found. Leastways, so I think.'

In mute response Josh indicated the grave and its offering of flowers that were even now closing their petals for the night.

'Violets! This proves it — Emma always did have a love for wayside blooms.' Alice was beside herself. 'Josh, I beg of you, listen to me.'

She told him about the visit to Rudge and what had transpired.

'Emma is currently engaged as house-keeper to one Mistress Rosamund Platt of Peckforton. The name of the house is Hillside.'

Josh shook his head.

'There's more to this than you can possibly imagine. Emma has certain blood ties.'

'The Dawnes, you mean? Pshaw! Hamilton told me about that.'

'They're gentry. Fish and fowl don't blend.'

'Oh, fie! Josh, you're worth ten of them. Please, don't throw away the chance of happiness. Not now when we are so close to finding her. You cannot know Emma's side of things.'

'I know enough,' Josh said harshly. 'I went to the shop, spoke with the brother. It's no use, Alice. I'm taking myself out of Emma's way. It's clearly too late now to set off. Best I put up overnight at the old place and leave tomorrow at first light.'

Alice looked at his set face and felt her heart sink. How infuriatingly stubborn men could be. How distressingly unbending.

'As you wish. But I'm warning you, Josh. This is a decision you will live to regret.'

She swung on her heel and walked away, leaving Josh standing there, his gaze returned in hopeless yearning to the posy of flowers by the headstone.

★   ★   ★

Home again, the horse stabled, Alice went inside to find to her faint consternation, her father waiting for her. His face was unsmiling.

'Papa? You are home early.'

'Indeed. Alice, a word if you please.'

He indicated his study. Meekly, her heart quailing, Alice entered the room with the dog clutched to her. Her father followed, closing the door behind them with a resounding click. There was no invitation to sit. He came purposefully to face her where she stood, uncertainly, in the middle of the green and gold patterned Turkish carpet.

'Alice, it has come to my ears that you were unfavourably involved in this unfortunate business with Emma Trigg.'

Alice felt the colour drain from her cheeks. She swallowed hard.

'Papa, I . . . '

'No excuses, miss. 'Tis written all over your face. Why, Alice? Emma was your friend. How could you?'

'It was because of Hamilton,' Alice blurted out. 'Papa, I love him.'

'Love? I doubt you know the meaning of the word! To think that a daughter of mine could be so deceitful and conniving! To go and deliberately make trouble for one so obviously innocent of wrongdoing. How dare you let your mama and me down in this way! Gideon Trigg is a fellow trader. I respect him, as he does me. Or did. As for your poor mama, she's taken to her bed with an attack of the megrims, so upset is she . . . '

On and on her father went, the angry words battering on Alice's brain. Tears spurted. Blindly she lowered the dog to the floor and fumbled in her reticule for her kerchief.

'Papa,' she stammered, once he had stopped for breath. 'In truth I have tried to put matters right. That's what I've been doing today. I spoke to Josh Brookfield but he wouldn't listen to me.'

'I'm not a whit surprised.' Her father was incensed. 'And I'll say this. If you are expecting a betrothal between you and young Catchpole after what has happened, Alice, you delude yourself. Think you the Triggs would endorse it once they know what you've done?'

'They do know. Leastways, Mistress Catchpole does. Hamilton put in a word for me.'

'Did he indeed! I'm telling you, miss, should that young man come to my door asking for your hand, the answer will be no.'

'Papa!'

'No! You can wait, be it five years or ten, until I consider you mature enough for matrimony. And think on this, Alice. Don't expect everyone to be as forgiving as the Catchpoles. Likely you and he will set up home and business away from here. It could be the making of Catchpole, to be apart from his mama. She pampers him, like I have you.

'Still, amends can be made. Instead of twiddling your thumbs at home you can come to the office and work for me. Happen it will stand you in good stead for the future. Catchpole will require some assistance with the paperwork, in business on his own. That will be all. Pray leave me.'

Contrite, Alice did so, unwittingly closing the door on the dog who gave a pitiful whimper for her mistress. In all likelihood, her pet was the only one in the Courtney household who wanted the company of Alice at that moment.

★　★　★

Emma fastened the pony to a tethering ring at Beeston market and threw a doubtful glance at the sky. The day had dawned bright but now clouds were gathering, hinting at rain before long.

'It's to be hoped we're not in for a drenching,' she said to the pony, who nudged her hand in the everlasting hope of titbits. 'Greedy! Here's a crust of bread. Be good until I get back.'

Emma collected her shopping basket from the trap and made her way through the ranks of parked farm carts, traps and carriages, the horses waiting patiently between the shafts, some whiling away the time with a tasty nosebag of oats.

Market days always had been a welcome change for Emma. She liked the throb and bustle of the crowds and the camaraderie of the stallholders, and there was always the chance of a chat with someone. Today she had left off her housekeeper's dress and put on one of the fashionable new outfits Rosamund Platt had insisted upon having made for her — a fetching sky-blue poplin with matching cape and delightful feathered hat.

The air resounded with the urgent calls of penned animals on the far side of the ground where the beast auction was held, and Emma was reminded sorrowfully of another market ten long months previously.

What changes there had been in that period. What heartache and disruption. Many times had she been forced to tell herself to count her blessings, and these had not been lacking of late. Nonetheless, the yearning in her heart had never quite gone away and Emma did not have to search very deeply to know why.

She consulted her shopping list. Threads, needles and ribbons for the mistress. Haberdasher's first then, after which she had best seek out a stall selling kitchen herbs and spices, Mrs Bates having been voluble over the need to replenish her shelf.

'Tarragon and dill and thyme a-plenty. Mercy me, I shan't be sorry to see it all sprouting again in the kitchen garden. Tes there then for the picking. You wunna forget, Emma lass?'

She had given Emma a broad smile, her face dimpling in affection, and Emma had made her assurances.

'No, Cook. I promise I won't forget.'

She set off, heading for the first port of call where a queue was already forming.

Shopping done, she took the laden basket back to the trap and, tempted by a stall of knick-knacks and fairings, she returned for a closer look. Before setting out the mistress — or Cousin Rosamund, as she would eventually be known — had pressed upon her a purse of coin, saying in tones that brooked no argument that it was for Emma's personal use.

A dainty blue jug had caught Emma's eye. She was debating on whether to take the plunge and buy the item, the purchasing of something for the pure pleasure of it being a new and terrifying experience, when she felt the first light drops of rain.

Mindful of her fine new clothes, she looked hastily around for somewhere to shelter. The rain worsened and there was a mass dive for cover. Emma gathered up her skirts and was about to join the scramble when she heard a voice ring out above the general din.

'Ah, to be sure now, what's a drop of rain? It's just the pride of the morning!'

Emma stopped in her tracks, her heart racing and throat suddenly gone dry.

'Josh?' she said shakily. 'Oh . . . Josh, it's you!'

'Emma.' He came striding up and took her

hands in his. 'Emma — thank God! I called at Hillside House. They told me I'd find you here. And here you are, after all this while. I can scarce believe it. Sweeting, I've searched endlessly for you. Your folks, too. We've all been desperate to find you. Where in heaven's name have you been all this time? Why hide away, like you clearly have been doing?'

Emma's mind went distressingly back to that dank day in October, waiting for him in vain at their trysting place in the hills. She had been so full of foolish hopes and dreams, but she was older now — older and wiser. She freed her hands from his.

'I waited but you didn't come,' she said in a low voice. 'I waited and waited. It grew dark and stormy and still you didn't come.'

'If you only knew the times I've reproached myself over that. Father was taken badly. I couldn't leave him. I left a note explaining what had happened, bidding you to trust me. It was unfortunate that you never received it. My other letters, too. Emma, there is so much you should know it's hard to work out where to begin. This I must say. There is someone of great importance to you at your grandfather's house who's longing to meet you.'

'There is? I don't understand.'

'No more should you. You will have to take my word on it.'

'Granfer Trigg and Aunt Maisie — they are well?'

'Aye, well enough. Your brother, too. And that hapless fool, Catchpole. God's truth, I swear he and that trouble-making little minx from the vintner's deserve each other.'

Emma bit her lip.

'Josh, the situation has changed. I'm not what you thought.'

'I know.' His look was tender.

'You don't mind that I'm . . . I'm baseborn?' She was hard put to say the word.

Josh shrugged.

'I minded more about your connections on your mama's side. I've sat half the night pondering on what to do for the best. The answer was always the same. Emma, I love you. Life without you would be meaningless. What happened in the past is beside the point. All that really matters is us — you and me and what we make of our life together.

'That is, if you will have me. I swear I shall look after you. You'll want for nothing. We shall have a home of our own choosing. It will have a shelf for your skillets and ladles and the stillroom you so wished for. Aye, and a few rod of ground to grow your plants. Whatever you need, only say we shall be together . . . Emma?'

Emma struggled to take in what he said. It seemed incomprehensible, and yet through it all one bright flame burned steadily. He did not mind about her questionable background. He loved her no matter what. Everything was going to be all right.

It was as if a great load had lifted from her shoulders, leaving her light-headed and filling slowly with an unimaginable relief and happiness. She gave him a tremulous smile.

Neither of them had noticed that the rain had stopped. The sun appeared, radiant and golden, glinting on the silver charms of the bracelet on her wrist. Church, wedding slipper, cottage, spinning wheel, cradle and tiny horse.

'There now,' Josh said, smiling, raindrops glistening in his mop of dark hair, 'if that little trinket hasn't worked its magic and brought us back together. Didn't I say it would bring luck?'

'So you did.'

Emma gazed at him in breathless, shining joy. He had come seeking her out. How fine and strong he was. How she loved him.

Without another word she stepped into his arms, laid her cheek against the rough fabric of his coat and stood there, safe in his embrace, where she had always wanted to be.

Around them the market bustled on, and high above the sun's rays strengthened, bringing warmth and promise for times to come.

We do hope that you have enjoyed reading this large print book.

Did you know that all of our titles are available for purchase?

We publish a wide range of high quality large print books including:
Romances, Mysteries, Classics
General Fiction
Non Fiction and Westerns

Special interest titles available in large print are:
The Little Oxford Dictionary
Music Book
Song Book
Hymn Book
Service Book

Also available from us courtesy of Oxford University Press:
Young Readers' Dictionary
(large print edition)
Young Readers' Thesaurus
(large print edition)

For further information or a free brochure, please contact us at:
Ulverscroft Large Print Books Ltd.,
The Green, Bradgate Road, Anstey,
Leicester, LE7 7FU, England.
Tel: **(00 44) 0116 236 4325**
Fax: **(00 44) 0116 234 0205**

Other titles published by Ulverscroft:

THE LONELY FURROW

Pamela Kavanagh

The collapse of the City of Glasgow Bank brings disaster to the Drummond family. They lose their business and place in society. Nathan's dream of an engineering career is ended, along with the betrothal to his beloved Isobel. When an unexpected inheritance saves the day, the Drummonds must leave their comfortable Glasgow home for a run-down farm in Shropshire. Chrissie, the maid, proves a godsend during difficult times, despite her secret love for Nathan. Can the family keep the shame of their past hidden? Will Nathan manage the farm and recognize love for the girl who keeps his family together?

ACROSS THE SANDS OF TIME

Pamela Kavanagh

Newly engaged to Geoff, schoolteacher Thea Partington is happy with her career, her show ponies and family life at their farm on the Wirral. But everything changes when Irish vet Dominic joins the local practice and Thea is attracted to him. The engaged pair begin to renovate an idyllic, but empty and ramshackle, property on Partington land. Thea experiences a series of waking dreams of the history of the house, revealing uncanny parallels, stormy relationships and fearful consequences. Meanwhile, Dominic, a man with a past, loves Thea, but believes he is fated. But are the fates on their side?

MOORLAND MIST

Gwen Kirkwood

Emma Greig has seen little of the world when she leaves school at fourteen to become a maid at Bonnybrae Farm, a life far removed from her carefree schooldays. The Sinclair family both welcomes and rejects her: Maggie is kind and warm; her brothers, Jim and William, playful. But the haughty Mrs Sinclair, disturbed by her children's friendship with a maid, resolves to remind Emma of her place in the world. When Emma and William defy her and strike up a closer bond, Emma is sent away — and William banished from the farm he loves . . .